DANGEROUS RAPTURE

It had been very kind and generous of Roma's godfather to leave her a valuable racehorse—but had he known what he was doing when he also stipulated that the horse should be trained by Earl Paget? For, quite apart from his maddening, authoritative ways, Earl was, Roma was sure, not being honest about the situation. But what could she do about it?

TUG OF WAR

There was absolutely no reason why Dee Lawrence's and Nat Archer's paths should cross—but somehow they did, to Dee's dismay and fury. For every time they met the sparks flew—and what was far worse, Nat always got the better of her. Why didn't he just *go away*?

MARRIAGE IN HASTE

Trapped in a Far Eastern country on the brink of civil war, Netta could only manage to escape if she married Joss de Courcy—a man she knew only by his reputation, as 'the Fox'. She didn't have much choice in the circumstances—but did he have to treat her as *quite* such a helpless idiot?

CLAWS OF A WILDCAT

'I travel alone. I can't be bothered with encumbrances—however attractive,' Dominic Orr had told Margaret uncompromisingly. But after all, she was a career girl too; her job as a doctor was just as important to her as his as a geologist on an oil rig was to him. So where was the problem?

SHADOW OF AN EAGLE

Why had Marion taken such an immediate and instinctive dislike to Reeve Harland when he turned up to stay in her peaceful valley home? It was almost as if she had some premonition of what he was there for. Yet she didn't know, for quite a long time—and by then it was too late . . .

DANGEROUS RAPTURE

BY

SUE PETERS

MILLS & BOON LIMITED
15–16 BROOK'S MEWS
LONDON W1A 1DR

First published 1981
Australian copyright 1981
Philippine copyright 1981
This edition 1981

© Sue Peters 1981

ISBN 0 263 73566 4

Set in Monophoto Baskerville 10 on 10½ pt.

*Made and printed in Great Britain by
Richard Clay (The Chaucer Press) Ltd,
Bungay, Suffolk*

CHAPTER ONE

'YOU'VE scratched my horse from the race!' Roma turned on him, her eyes blazing. 'You've taken Silver Cloud out of the running. You've got no right!' she stormed at him furiously.

'As the horse's trainer, I've got every right,' he answered her curtly, and added, 'you shouldn't need reminding that under the terms of the will, I've got *sole* right over the destiny of the filly for the next two years. And in my opinion,' he added deliberately, 'the going on the course today is far too heavy for Cloud to put up a good performance.'

'And I suppose, in your opinion,' she stressed sarcastically, 'the going, however heavy, is just right for Arabian Minty?'

He was allowing his own horse to race, she saw bitterly. In fact, three of the horses from his stables were among the runners lining up even now to be put into the starting stalls—his own big chestnut gelding with the white blaze on its face, and two more animals he was training for other owners. There were eight runners in the field altogether, Roma saw. There should have been nine. Silver Cloud would have been the only grey among the line-up.

'Heavy going doesn't worry Minty, he's an older horse, with more stamina. Cloud's only a two-year-old, and more lightly built. So far as your filly's concerned, this race was only a trial to see what her staying power is like. She'd probably flounder on the soft going, and I don't intend to risk exhausting her for the sake of an unimportant race. I want her in tip-top condition for the rest of the season.'

The race might seem unimportant to Earl; it was just the reverse to herself. 'Cloud won at Newmarket last week,' she persisted stubbornly.

'It was a novices' race, and the going was good,' Earl retorted impatiently. 'The turf at Newmarket last week was firm and dry, and not too hard.'

And Silver Cloud had seemed to fly along. It was the first race meeting she had ever attended, and Roma could not believe the speed of the contestants. The excitement of it gripped her still. And afterwards. . . . Her eyes glowed at the memory of afterwards. Nothing she had ever experienced before could equal the thrill of receiving the trophy Silver Cloud had won; of leading her horse into the winner's enclosure, and receiving congratulations as the owner. And since then, anticipation had built up in her at the prospect of the race today. She hardly dared to think, to hope. . . .

She turned away, sick disappointment blurring the distant line-up of horses at the starting post. 'The going isn't all that bad,' she muttered to herself rebelliously. She poked the toe of her shoe against the turf, experimentally. The ground was soft, very soft from the heavy rain of the night before, but from the way Earl spoke, anyone would think it was a quagmire, she thought angrily.

'They're off!'

The crowd roared suddenly, and startled her eyes into clarity again, in time to see the line of horses shoot out from their starting stalls like bullets from a gun.

'I won't watch. I don't even want to see his wretched horse. . . .'

But she could not turn away. In spite of her resolve, her eyes seemed to glue themselves to the struggle for supremacy taking place on the course ahead.

'Arabian Minty! Arabian Minty!'

The crowd around her went mad with excitement, and even from this distance Roma could see clods of earth flying from under the racing hooves. The going was softer than she had realised. In her ignorance, she had not understood the powerful cutting force of metal shoes on rain-soaked turf. But even that did not excuse Earl from scratching her horse from the race without first consulting her.

'I hope Minty loses,' she wished uncharitably.

The big chestnut gelding lay fourth. Roma could pick out the stable colours quite easily with her naked eye, the orange vest and black sleeves stood out against the reds and blues and striped armbands of the other jockeys.

'Arabian Minty!'

The crowd cheered their favourite on, and Roma wondered whether the horse could hear its name, and understand. Or whether, more likely, Mick the stable jockey, the man with the child-sized body and the rich Kerry brogue, urged his mount to greater effort. Slowly the chestnut overhauled the third horse, then the second, and with long, raking strides started to catch up with the leader, a big black horse ridden by a jockey with red and white armbands. Roma caught her breath, unable to help the excitement that surged up in her, determined not to let Earl see. Reason told her his decision not to let Cloud run was right. Resentment at his arrogance in not consulting her, as the owner, first, made her boil inwardly.

'It would serve him right if Minty loses!'

But it seemed as if her uncharitable wish was not to be granted. The big chestnut caught up with the black, and the two raced neck and neck. Roma risked a glance behind her. She need not have bothered to hide her feelings, she thought crossly, piqued in spite of herself because Earl would not have noticed her expression anyway. He had his fieldglasses to his eyes, and trained them unwaveringly on the track. Assessing Minty's chances. Assessing the chestnut's performance. Gathering information that would tell him what further schooling was needed, and where and when to race the gelding again. He stood perfectly still, unmoving except for the slow sweep of his fieldglasses, following the racing horses.

'The man's made of stone,' Roma thought scornfully. As Minty's owner, he should be cheering his horse on. She felt like cheering herself, and suppressed the inclination ruthlessly. 'I won't let him see,' she vowed, but her hands gripped the rail in front of her until their knuckles turned white. The chestnut and the black were only yards from the winning line. The black seemed to be labouring. It had reached the peak of its performance, and could produce nothing more, but the chestnut still had speed in reserve, and with a final burst it forged ahead, and passed the winning post half a length ahead of its rival, to the delighted cheers of the crowd.

'Good on yer, Minty!'

The nearby punter must be a tourist. His unrestrained joy, as well as his broad Australian accent, turned more than one amused face in his direction from the vocal but slightly more restrained English crowd of racegoers surrounding him. A reluctant smile touched the corners of Roma's lips as she watched him punch his hat back into shape, and clap it on his head. During the race, the unfortunate headgear had been slapped against his knee, beaten flat, and hammered on top of the rails in its owner's excitement—not for the first time, Roma guessed shrewdly; the battered felt looked as if it had endured a good deal of such treatment. She sent it a sympathetic glance as it disappeared among the milling crowd, sheltering its wearer's broad grin.

'Anyone would think he was Minty's owner, instead of Earl.' The Australian had shown a good deal more enthusiasm than her companion, and expended a lot more breath on cheering on the chestnut, than had Earl, she thought critically.

'Let's go.'

The trainer slipped his fieldglasses back into their case, closed the fastener with a sharp snap, and took Roma's arm as if nothing untoward had occurred. His unemotional demeanour roused the anger in her that seemed always to lurk beneath the surface whenever she was with Earl. She longed to shout at him,

'Say something. *Do* something. At least *look* as if you're pleased your horse has won!'

The arrogance of the man! she thought angrily. His cool calm seemed to be a tacit acceptance that, because it was his horse, it could not do anything else but win. It should have been Cloud. . . . She swallowed hard, and in as even a voice as she could manage, said,

'Go? Where to?'

'The winners' enclosure, of course.'

'There's no "of course" about it,' she thought irritably as he guided her through the throng of people. All this was new to her. Breeding and training race horses was Earl's living, the racecourses a part of his working life. He knew just what to do, and where to go.

'He would have been just as bewildered as I am, if he'd tried being an air hostess,' she comforted herself. The thought of Earl Paget as an air hostess twitched her lips upwards again. The blue fodder cap of her recently handed-in uniform would have sat oddly on her companion's brown, wavy hair, uncompromisingly cut short and brushed back away from his lean brown face, out of the way of the keen brown glance that seemed to have an uncomfortable habit of reading her very thoughts. Reading her very private thoughts, in a manner she found disconcerting, and daily more disturbing. She turned her mind hastily back to her uniform.

The forage cap was nice, she thought wistfully. It had sat at a jaunty angle atop her neat cap of curly dark hair, flirted with the upturned dark lashes covering rather serious grey eyes that lit up with a delicious sparkle when she smiled, and pointed back at her cheekily retroussé nose. It was her own fault that she had handed in her cap and uniform. She had been eager enough to do so at the time, she remembered ruefully.

'You'll regret it,' Jane, her second in the flight, warned her. Then, 'You're not by any chance running away because of Flip Dean, are you?' she questioned shrewdly.

'Good heavens, no,' Roma laughed, all the more merrily because she knew, happily, she spoke the truth. Flip, of the toothpaste advert good looks, stunningly handsome in his pilot's uniform, and aware of it, Roma acknowledged amusedly, Flip was the darling of the air hostesses, had squired each one in turn, and was taken seriously by none. Certainly not by herself.

It had been fun while it lasted, she acknowledged, but

it was like icing on a cake, sweet and insubstantial, and it ended after a few hectic weeks without regret on either side. She still had Flip's parting gift in her room, a tiny phial of expensive French perfume, which typically was to the pilot's taste and not to her own. She had used it only once, on their last evening out together. It was exotic, glamorous, and redolent of the brittle, sophisticated leisure life the pilot loved. And which she did not, she admitted candidly, and stuffed it into the back of her suitcase, where it had remained ever since.

'If you're not nursing a broken heart, why leave the airline?' Jane was puzzled, and showed it. 'You can't live without an income,' she persisted, 'and it's no good relying on a racehorse to provide you with one,' she warned Roma seriously.

'I know, and I don't. I wouldn't be so silly.'

'If you give up your flat, you'll have nowhere to live,' Jane went on relentlessly. 'Fancy anyone leaving you a derelict lodge, and a racehorse which for all you know might be derelict as well. How are you going to look after the beast?' Her tone suggested that Roma was not capable, in her present mood, of looking after herself.

It was not fancy, it was fact, Roma thought, but before she could draw breath to reply, Jane hurried on,

'Where is this lodge place, anyway? And if you can't live in it until it's repaired, where will you go? Country pubs can be expensive on a long-term basis,' she pressed anxiously, her mind obviously still running on Roma's current lack of a regular income.

'The Lodge is the one to Burdon Court, near the village of Down Burdon,' Roma explained patiently. 'The executors are going to have it restored before I take it over, and until then they've arranged with the owner that I shall live in Burdon Court itself. It should only be for a matter of a month or so.'

'That's a relief!' Jane let out an exaggerated sigh. 'It means the Court is habitable, even if the Lodge isn't. I take it that the Court *is* habitable?' she asked suspiciously.

'It's being lived in,' Roma assured her. 'My godfather left the Court to his nephew.'

'Oh, so there's a nephew?' Jane perked up with unashamed interest.

'We've never met,' Roma began.

'You didn't know your godfather very well, either, from the sound of it,' her friend said critically.

'That wasn't his fault,' Roma excused her benefactor. 'He lived abroad because of his wife's health, and so did we. Having a diplomat for a father has its disadvantages,' she admitted ruefully. 'We lived in every country of the world except our own, and somehow we never seemed to be in the same country as my godfather at the same time. I think the last time I saw him was when I was about four years old. And as for his nephew, apparently he's a racehorse trainer. He's got his training stables and a stud at Burdon Court. There's a lot of ground to the place, and the downs are nearby, and make ideal galloping for his string. And he's looking after my horse for me,' she answered her friend's earlier question.

'Oh, a racehorse trainer.' Jane lost interest. 'You'll be safe enough staying with him,' she predicted gloomily. 'He'll be bandy-legged, and wear a frightful hacking jacket, and probably have a horsey-faced wife with a tweed skirt that bags at the knees, and a row of beads as long as a prayer string.'

The fine tweed of his hacking jacket was impeccably cut, and his legs were long, and straight. And there was no sign of a wife. With a scowl as black as the one he bent upon herself, Roma had her doubts that anyone would want to marry him anyway. She guessed his identity the moment she saw him. His educated voice, his authoritative manner—arrogant manner, Roma told herself indignantly—pointed to him being the owner of Burdon Court. But not of the Lodge, she reminded herself firmly, and faced him with her chin held high.

'You're trespassing,' he accused her brusquely.

'I came to see the Lodge.' Roma stood her ground in the wilderness that was the front garden.

'It's not for sale.'

'I know. . . .'

'Burdon Court is private property,' he went on, as if she had not spoken, she thought resentfully. 'No one, except for myself and my staff, has any right of access to the grounds.'

'Except for the owner of the Lodge,' she got in at last, evenly.

'The owner is abroad somewhere.' He dismissed her words with an impatient gesture. 'I intend to purchase the Lodge and have it restored to house a member of my staff.'

The cool effrontery of the man took her breath away. He was disposing of her part of the legacy without even a 'by your leave'! Doubtless he thought if she was safely abroad he could do whatever he liked with her property, and get away with it. 'The cheek of it!' she thought furiously. It was obvious he had been on a tour of inspection of the house, he had come round the corner of it on a side path leading onto the main path on which she stood. The Lodge was not his to inspect. 'And never will be,' she vowed determinedly.

Seconds before Earl Paget appeared, she was contemplating the possibility of asking the executors to sell the Lodge for whatever they could get. Her dismayed appraisal suggested it would not be for very much. The house did not appear to have been lived in for a long time. The roof sagged under ancient thatch that looked as if it might offer sanctuary to all sorts of creepy-crawlies, she thought shudderingly. And the garden would need a bulldozer and a gang of navvies to restore order to the wild tangle of thicket covering what probably had once been neat borders.

'I am the owner,' she stated in a clear voice, and had the satisfaction of seeing his eyebrows raised in a surprised stare. 'And I've got no intention of selling my property to anyone,' she added deliberately. 'As soon as the Lodge is made habitable, I shall live here myself.' She made sure he had no lingering doubts about her intentions.

'I was told you were an air hostess.' He recovered remarkably quickly, she thought with grudging admiration. 'Of what possible use can a home in Down Burdon be to you? The nearest commercial airport is all of forty miles away.'

He had a point there, but he was not to know she was no longer an air hostess. Some instinct of caution warned Roma to keep the knowledge to herself. If he once learned of her jobless state, it would give him a lever to press her to sell him the Lodge.

'Forty miles isn't all that far,' she said airily, ignoring the fact that she did not own a car. 'And if the travelling becomes inconvenient, I can always use the house as a weekend and holiday home,' she finished carelessly, deliberately rubbing in the fact that the Lodge was her own to use or only half use, just as she chose. She stopped speaking, and waited, and knew swift disappointment that his only reaction to her barb was an extra steely quality in his already hostile stare.

'He'll fight to get his own way.' Her fellow legatee would make a formidable adversary, she thought with quick insight, and momentarily she felt a prick of uneasiness. She rallied quickly. 'If he fights, I'll fight back,' she promised herself staunchly, and across the disputed threshold defiant grey eyes met determined brown ones in a silent declaration of hostilities, which ever since had flared into a renewed skirmish every time she and Earl were together.

'I intend to have the Lodge,' he told her bluntly at dinner that evening, when he had reluctantly honoured his agreement with the executors to house her under his own roof until the Lodge was made habitable. 'The place goes with Burdon Court, and it should be put to the use for which it was originally intended, to house staff. Not to be used as an occasional holiday retreat; as a toy,' he said scornfully. 'A caravan on the coast would be cheaper to run, if a holiday home is all you want. Maintaining a cottage just for the sake of an occasional weekend would be expensive, even for an air hostess,' he added with a

sarcastic inflection that brought a flush of anger to warm
Roma's cheeks.

'I'll pay for it from the money Silver Cloud earns by
winning races,' she flashed back swiftly. 'If you live up to
your supposed reputation as a trainer, there should be
sufficient income from winnings to keep the Lodge comfortably,' she taunted him, and could have laughed out
loud at the delicious irony of it, that Earl's own efforts
might finance the very thing he wished to wrest from her.

Which might be the reason why he had scratched Silver
Cloud from today's race. The thought stopped Roma in
her tracks. The trainer was fighting her with weapons she
could not match. Bitterly now she wished she had not
given way to the temptation to goad him, but the words
had been spoken, and they could not be recalled. They
held an extra significance now, which at all costs Earl
must not learn about, she thought worriedly. Under no
circumstances must he find out that she had left her job,
that she might actually need any winnings her horse might
be fortunate enough to earn for her, to help her to main-
tain her new home. Her savings would not last for ever,
but once she was safely installed in the Lodge, Earl would
not be in such a good position to put pressure on her to
sell it to him. While she was under his roof she was vulnerable, but when she was living in her own home she
could cast about for another source of income at her leisure. Working from home as a freelance interpreter was
one possibility, she thought hopefully. The idea was attractive. Air hostessing had been fun, but lately she discovered a hitherto unexpected longing to put down roots,
and live a life that offered some kind of stability instead of
the endless prospect of being in Paris one day, Tokyo the
next, New York the next. . . .

'I've roamed the world for as long as I can remember,'
she confessed to the worried Jane when she first broke the
news that she intended to leave the airline. 'First it was
with my parents, and then with my job. Now I want to
be able to stay in one place, to make friends instead of
just passing acquaintances.'

'Roaming the world has given you fluent command of six languages,' Jane pointed out to her drily, and first put the idea of freelance interpreting into her mind.

'There's no time now to stand daydreaming,' Earl said impatiently, and tightened his grip on her arm, forcing her to carry on walking beside him. 'I've got to get to the winners' enclosure in time to lead Minty in.'

If Cloud had raced, it might have been Roma who was to lead in the winner. She glanced up at the trainer, her newly awakened suspicion darkening her forehead with a frown, but Earl was not looking at her, he was looking ahead, busily steering a way through the milling crowd, to where the horses that took part in the race were already filing back from past the winning post.

'How did he go?' he asked the jockey when they came abreast. No congratulations. No, 'Well done!' Roma noticed. The least Earl could do would be to congratulate Mick on winning the race, she thought critically. She smiled up at the jockey, perched like a small leprechaun on top of the chestnut—an extra sweet smile to compensate for Earl's delinquency.

'He went like a train,' Mick responded enthusiastically. 'He's not even blowing.'

The black horse was richly lathered, Roma saw, but Arabian Minty showed no signs of distress.

'It was heavy going, though,' the little Irishman went on ruefully. 'Look what they've done to my nice clean silks!' he mourned. He was heavily spattered with mud, Roma saw, startled. His silk blouse, even his face. 'Minty and I *had* to get in front of the others, so as to stay reasonably clean,' he joked.

'Let's get the horse rugged up, and you into the weighing room.' With one hand Earl reached up for the bridle, and Roma tried to step back, to free herself from his grasp. It was adding insult to injury, she thought resentfully, to be forced to accompany him, when it should have been herself leading in the winner.

'Stay with me, or you'll get lost in the crowd.'

Was he concerned about her being lost, or was he

deliberately rubbing salt into her wound? she wondered bitterly, and then found herself unexpectedly glad of the support of his hand as a surge of people surrounded them. A chorus of voices called out congratulations to Earl, congratulating Mick. Making up for the trainer's unemotional acceptance of the jockey's efforts, she thought thankfully. A clutch of what she afterwards learned were racing journalists closed in on them and clicked cameras right in their faces. Roma expected the gelding to show signs of nervousness, but to her surprise the horse seemed to revel in the fuss, as if it knew that it had achieved something wonderful, and accepted the acclaim that followed as nothing more than its rightful due.

'It's as bad as its master,' Roma told herself tartly. She had not realised before that horses could be vain. Her acquaintance with riding school hacks had taught her the basics of horsemanship, but not a great deal about the horses themselves. A bubble of laughter rose up in her as she watched Minty's ears prick forward, and saw the animal actually preen itself in front of the press cameras. The laughter burst forth in a merry peal as she caught the newsman's eye, and an answering smile lit Earl's face, an indulgent smile for his favourite, not for herself, she thought sourly. Whenever Earl looked in her direction, his expression was either angry, frowning or critical.

She glanced up at him, curious to see what change a smile had wrought on the normally stern face she was accustomed to. His teeth gleamed white against his bronzed skin, and his whole face was relaxed. He looked younger, carefree.

'Handsome,' she thought with an unexpected sense of shock. Not in the way that Flip Dean had been handsome. The latter's good looks owed a great deal to his youth and his uniform. Earl's looks were different. They were fine-boned, enduring, and strong. 'Thoroughbred' was the word that ran through her mind, and she checked her thoughts sharply. Earl was beginning to occupy them far too often. She disliked him, she told herself sharply, mistrusted him. 'But however hard she tried, she could not

ignore him. Against her will a constant, growing awareness of him invaded her peace of mind, trespassing on the
privacy of her innermost thoughts in a manner she
resented and began to fear, but which she seemed helpless
to prevent. As if he sensed she was watching him, he
looked down, and she drew in her breath sharply, taken
unawares as she found herself looking up directly into his
eyes.

'They're flecked,' she discovered. Some detached awareness in her noticed the brown eyes were flecked, like peat
pools caught by dappled sunlight, deep, mysterious, with-
holding their secrets from the passer by. She stared
upwards, mesmerised, unable to draw her own eyes away,
at once fascinated and frightened, compelled to try to read
the secrets in his enigmatic stare, and at the same time
longing to clasp her hands over her own eyes, to shut
herself away from the masterful, compelling quality of his
look that turned her will to water, and made her long to
run away and hide, but confusedly she did not know
whether she wanted to hide away from Earl's look, or
from herself.

'That's fine. Hold it.'

Someone called out to her, but she only half heard the
call. She could not move if she wanted to, she thought
helplessly. There was a blinding flash, a sharp mechanical
click, and the spell was broken. Roma looked away, dazed
and shaking, in time to see the newspaper man hasten
away to catch his early edition, with Earl's look and her
own captured in his camera for posterity.

CHAPTER TWO

AND for publication. Roma opened the newspaper the
next morning, and stared down at the photograph with
mounting horror.

'It's a real bonny picture.' Mrs Murray, the Burdon

Court housekeeper, beamed her approval as she served Roma with breakfast.

'It looks like a wedding photograph,' the subject of it realised, appalled. 'If the airline staff see this, they'll think I've inherited a romance, as well as a racehorse!' Had she? Before her thoughts could go any farther along that particular line she switched them off, hurriedly. 'I look like an infatuated schoolgirl,' she told herself in disgust.

It was said that a camera could not lie. She studied her own pictured face, and her heart began to beat with slow, painful thuds. Earl's expression was cool, amused, giving nothing away. Her own. . . . She gulped. Bewitched was the only word that adequately described it. Her hand shook, making the newspaper rustle, and she dropped it on to the tablecloth from nerveless fingers.

The photograph was a good one. Unlike most casual newspaper shots, it was clear—and cruelly revealing. It betrayed her innermost feelings, whose existence until now she had managed to hide, even from herself. The photograph declared them to the world as clearly as a town crier, she thought with dismay.

Betrayed, by her own face!

She sat back suddenly in her chair, her coffee spoon dropping with a clatter into her saucer, and a wave of faintness passed over her as another thought struck her like a lightning bolt, blotting out all else.

If the photograph brought her so ruthlessly face to face with her own feelings, might it not also betray how she felt to Earl? And if so. . . . Another thought followed rapidly upon the first. If he guessed, which heaven forbid! she told herself fervently, but it was there for any discerning eye to see, and she could not prevent the trainer from looking at his morning paper. If he guessed, would he use the knowledge as another lever, to prise the Lodge from her possession?

She sat up again, suddenly, and took a hasty gulp from her coffee cup. In one unguarded moment she had handed Earl another deadly weapon in his fight for possession of her inheritance, and she did not doubt that he would have no hesitation in using it, if once he realised it was his. The hot black liquid steadied her, and she drew in a long, careful breath, and said as evenly as she could manage,

'Has Earl seen the paper yet?'

Perhaps it had not been delivered when he sat down for his own breakfast, she thought hopefully. He always ate very early, long before she herself came downstairs. Stable inspection was started by seven o'clock, and in the brief few days in which she had been the trainer's guest—unwelcome guest, she admitted wryly—she had not known him to be late. By now—she glanced at her wrist watch—the stable lads would be getting the string of horses ready for morning exercise.

'Oh yes,' Mrs Murray destroyed her hope almost before it was formed. 'He's taken his copy of the paper to the stable office, the same as he always does. He pins up the racing results on the notice board for the stable boys,' she added informatively, 'and then afterwards the information is all recorded in the log book he keeps for each horse.'

'He mustn't pin up my photograph. I won't let him,' Roma breathed in agitation. 'If he does, I'll tear it down,' she promised herself furiously. 'I won't have a moment's silliness emblazoned on a notice board for the amusement of the stable staff!' She tried to convince herself that it was only a moment's silliness, born of the excitement of the race, the strangeness of her surroundings, the whole upheaval of her life since she had learned of her inheritance. And since she had met Earl? She closed her mind to what had happened to her life since she first met Earl.

'I'm going to the stables,' she told Mrs Murray, and picked up her copy of the morning paper. She did not know quite how to get to the stables, she had not been there before, but she could see them from her bedroom window, and knew roughly the direction she would have to take.

'You'll need a woolly on,' the housekeeper warned her, 'there's a sharp nip in the air this morning.'

Roma did not feel like waiting to collect a woolly. She

wanted to rush down to the stable yard right away and confront Earl, to make him destroy the offending photograph, and never mind about trivialities like keeping warm. The way she felt now, she thought grimly, she had no,need of extra warmth; the events of the last few days had brought her to boiling point, and kept her there. But Mrs Murray was watching, expecting Roma to take her well-meant advice. She hesitated.

'The air can be bitterly cold in the down country, first thing in the morning,' the housekeeper noticed her hesitation. 'You don't want a cold to spoil your holiday here, do you?' she asked with motherly concern.

So Mrs Murray, too, thought she was only here for a brief holiday. No doubt the housekeeper took it for granted that if Earl wanted her to sell him the Lodge, she would do so without any argument. The older woman's casual acceptance that what the trainer wanted he would automatically get raised her temperature several notches higher, and made the thought of even the lightest woolly well nigh unendurable.

She nearly said, 'What holiday?' and checked herself just in time. Mrs Murray did not know, any more than did Earl, that her holiday from the airline was a permanent one, and that she was a fixture at Burdon Court until she was able to take possession of the Lodge.

'I'll go upstairs and put on a sweater.' To satisfy the housekeeper, she tucked the newspaper under her arm and mounted the stairs to her room. Her lightweight black slacks should be warm enough, but if it was as cold outside as Mrs Murray said, in spite of the bright October sunshine, then her sleeveless white silk shirt was guaranteed to cool her temper more quickly even than ripping down the offending photograph from the stable office notice board would do, if Earl had put it there. She threw the newspaper on to her bed and reached into a chest of drawers, and in a few seconds she had wriggled into a thin, pale blue woollen sweater, and tugged it down over her slacks top.

'That should be warm enough.' With a quick flip she

neatened her shirt collar over the top of the woolly, then reached for her hairbrush. 'I don't want to be all mussed up when I tackle Earl,' she murmured to herself. When she met up with the trainer she would need all the confidence she could muster, and the delay while she came upstairs did not help, she discovered with a qualm. If she had given way to her impulse and rushed off directly from the breakfast table without giving herself time to think, she could have confronted him, even had a blazing row with him and enjoyed it, she told herself confidently. Coming upstairs for her woolly *had* given her time to think, to wonder what she would do if Earl refused to allow her to touch his notice board, even refused to allow her entry into his stable office.

'I wish I'd never inherited the Lodge, or the racehorse,' she muttered rebelliously. If she had not been a legatee under her godfather's will, she would never have encountered Earl. If she had not met Earl, her normally calm, rational approach to life would not have been subjected to the devasting storms of the last few days, in which doubt and denial, defiant rejection of her own feelings, and tears of acceptance, had combined to wreck her sleep at night and ruin her appetite during the day. If she had done as Jane suggested and simply given instructions to the solicitors to sell the Lodge and the racehorse, she thought wistfully, she could have retained her post with the airline, and her path and Earl's would never have crossed.

'If—if—if. . . .' she thought impatiently. 'If wishes were horses, then beggars would ride!' The peculiar appropriateness of the old saw tilted her lips in a wry smile. 'I'm not exactly a beggar—yet,' she told herself stoutly, 'and at least my horse is a thoroughbred.' She turned to face the mirror, and raised her hairbrush.

'Oh, my goodness!' Her reflection looked back at her with wide-eyed dismay. 'You look like a schoolgirl in that outfit,' she told it disgustedly. The neat collared simplicity of pale blue and white took ten years off her age, just when she wanted, above all things, to look poised, and mature, and absolutely sure of herself. And yet—she glanced at her watch—if she wanted to see Earl before the string moved off at exercise, there was no time in which to change her clothes. The riders would be away for some time, and when they, and Earl, returned, the impact of her demand would be dissipated, and the stable staff would have had ample time to digest every detail of the photograph, and to draw their own conclusions. If she did not go now, she might as well not go at all.

'Flip's perfume!'

Inspiration came to her rescue, and she dived into the bedroom cupboard in search of her suitcase. 'I'm sure I put it in here somewhere. Ah, here it is.' Her fingers found the familiar knobbly feel of the cut glass phial, and she pulled it out triumphantly. 'It's just what I need.' Eagerly she pulled off the small gold cap and gave an experimental sniff. The perfume wafted round her, exotic, glamorous and exciting, subtly suggesting a woman-of-the-world, soignée sophistication that should easily combat the unwanted youthful appearance of her outfit, she thought with satisfaction. She wielded the spray with a liberal hand, wrinkled her nose in disgust at the cloying result, and hurried downstairs again before she could change her mind and wash it off.

'I wonder which way . . . ?'

Men's voices, and the sounds of busy activity, led her in the right direction, and in spite of herself her spirits rose as she crossed the garden in the crisp, bright morning air. She was only just in time, she saw, as she paused at the entrance to the stable yard. Already boys were leading horses out of stable doors, ready to take the string out for exercise. Incredibly small boys—apprentice jockeys. They looked much too small to have charge of such huge animals, but most of the thoroughbreds followed their lads obediently enough. A bevy of horses at the rear of the string were behaving in a rather lawless fashion, Roma noticed, giving their particular lads more trouble than the others. She hoped she had not got to pass them to get to the stable office.

'If you're looking for the Guv'nor, Miss Roma, he's in the stable office,' Steve, the head lad, called out to her, and added, 'He's on the phone just now, he'll be all of five minutes, I expect.'

It was no use confronting Earl while he was talking on the telephone. Roma bit her lip vexedly. He would have every excuse to ignore her, and she had no doubt he would use it to keep her waiting, like a naughty schoolgirl waiting outside the headmistress's study to be reprimanded for some misdemeanour.

'I won't give him that satisfaction,' she told herself crossly, and turned with relief when Steve offered,

'Come and speak to Silver Cloud, before I take her out. You ought to make friends with her, you'll be leading her into the winners' enclosure at a lot of the racecourses in the future, with a bit of luck,' the head lad encouraged.

'She might have had a chance yesterday,' Roma began discontentedly, and Steve shook his head.

'Not with the going as heavy as it was, she wouldn't. The Guv'nor did right to scratch her, she'd have tired herself out and lost condition, and the National Hunt season starts in a couple of weeks. That's the hurdling and the steeplechasing,' he took pity on Roma's blank look, and added, 'The flat racing is only for the summer months, from April until October. After that, the real racing begins,' he said enthusiastically. 'It's over the sticks, and away. . . .'

Her godfather's legacy had opened a door for her into a strange new world, but she was learning fast. She patted Arabian Minty, the hero of yesterday, and stolled across to where Steve was fussing about her own grey filly.

'She's beautiful.' The horse was all she had imagined her to be, and more. She was the only grey among the string, lightly dappled on her quarters, with a darker mane and tail. Silver Cloud aptly described her, and a thrill of pure joy shot through Roma as she put out a hand to rub the big nose.

'No airliner can possibly compare with this,' she told herself jubilantly.

The gracefully arched neck stretched the big head towards her. Two long ears pricked forward, and large,
luminous dark eyes regarded her with friendly curiosity.

'I still can't believe she's really mine.' Suddenly Roma
felt awestruck by the responsibility of her legacy. Earl
had control of the horse for the next two years, but Cloud
still belonged to her, Roma reminded herself firmly. After
the two years was up, she could do what she liked with
the horse. Even send her to another trainer, if she wanted
to. The thought boosted her morale slightly and enabled
her to give her attention to what Steve was saying.

'The glamour of the silks will catch up with you yet,'
the head lad promised. 'Cloud's entered to race in France
soon, at Auteuil, and after that there's Kempton Park,
and Newbury, and Cheltenham. We'll have you shopping
for a gorgeous hat for Ascot before you know where you
are,' he teased her with a smile.

'That'll be a long time away yet, I expect, but it'll be
nice to look forward to,' Roma laughed. 'At least Cloud's
got a good omen to start with!' She bent down and picked
up a young black cat that twined itself fearlessly around
the grey's hooves. 'You'll get stepped on if you do that,'
she scolded, and stroked the silky black handful into a
purr.

'Cloud won't step on Satan,' Steve reassured her.
'Those two are practically inseparable. The cat was born
in the filly's box, and they've struck up a friendship ever
since.'

'They make an odd pair.' Roma watched with growing
amazement as the horse thrust a gentle muzzle towards
the cat in her arms, which instead of taking fright as she
expected, simply reached out two miniature black paws
and playfully boxed its enormous companion.

'Animals strike up some odd friendships,' Steve agreed.
'We've had to cut a hinged flap in the stable door so that
the cat can come and go as it pleases. The filly gets restless
if Satan's away for too long, though. It's a bit like a child
missing its favourite teddy bear, I suppose,' he said indul-
gently.

'If Cloud's careful where she treads, the other horses
might not be.'

Roma's eyes widened with dismay as the cat suddenly
slid from her arms with quicksilver speed, attracted by a
handful of windblown straw that tumbled past them across
the stable yard. The bundle of dried corn stalks rustled
enticingly, and the young cat scampered after it like a
small black shadow, bouncing under the horse and out of
reach of Roma's hand.

'It'll get trodden on,' she cried anxiously, her own
errand to the stable yard temporarily forgotten. 'Those
horses at the back aren't standing quiet, like Cloud.'

'The colts are always a bit livelier than the fillies.
Don't get close to them, Miss Roma, you're wearing. . . .'

She did not wait to hear the rest of what Steve said.
Her whole attention was on the playing cat. One of the
rear horses, a black one with a white sock, reared high
and came down again on all fours with an alarming clatter
of hooves, and fear for the little animal galvanised Roma
into pursuit.

'Puss, puss, puss. . . .' She ran round Cloud to the other
side. 'Got you!' she exclaimed triumphantly, but the
breeze foiled her. With a tantalising puff it sent the tangle
of straw rolling on again, and the cat leapt after it, evading
her hand by a whisker. The little animal followed its
quarry fearlessly along the string of horses, and Roma
followed the cat, and the clatter of the black colt's hooves
drowned Steve's sharp call,

'Miss Roma. . . .'

Four or five of the horses at the back of the string were
still giving the stable lads trouble. Lively head-tossings
and cavortings milled them about like a group of unruly
schoolboys, sharpening Roma's fear for the cat, so that
she lost her own nervousness, and darted uncaring among
the restless group, intent on rescue.

'Clear off, Satan! Psssst!' The lad holding on to the
reins of the big black colt gave a sharp hiss through his
teeth, and sent the cat scuttling from under the black's

feet. The little animal abandoned its plaything, and leapt spitting on to the bottom half of an open loose box door, safely out of harm's way, and Roma stopped short. The cat was safe enough now. But was she? Her arrival among the colts seemed to trigger off a spate of even more lawless behaviour. The entire goup at the rear end of the string seemed to redouble its restless prancing, and pandemonium broke loose around her.

'Steady on, there, can't you? Whoa!'

An exasperated order rent the air as a second horse reared, and lifted its stable lad half off his feet in the process.

'Get back, miss! Get away, out of it,' the lad implored Roma urgently.

She spun round, thoroughly frightened now, and found there was nowhere she could get away to. Her pursuit of the cat had taken her right into the middle of the bunch of colts. Her only line of retreat was a small gap to one side, and even as she darted towards it, the black colt swung across it, blocking her way, and lashed out with vicious hooves. She turned back, cowering away from the kicking animal. It presented a fearsome spectacle to her alarmed stare, the whites of its eyes gleamed in stark contrast to its jet head, and it snorted loudly, nostrils flaring as it reared again, its forefeet threshing the air within an inch of Roma's head.

She stood petrified, unable to turn either way. Surely one small cat could not have upset such big animals? She had heard of elephants being stampeded by a mouse, but the cat was part of the life of the stables, and the horses must be accustomed to seeing it around.

The clatter, and the snorting, and the huge, jostling bodies rose to a terrifying crescendo around her. Urgent, 'Whoa's!' and, 'Back down there's,' from the beleagured stable lads added to the noise and confusion, and cutting across it from somewhere towards the head of the string, Roma heard Steve shout,

'Guv'nor, quick! Among the colts. . . .'

Hurrying footsteps made their way towards her. Even

amid the clatter of iron-shod hooves on cobbles, Roma knew the footsteps belonged to Earl.

'Move over, there!' He dodged the lashing hooves, thrust the black to one side with a muscular push against the mighty quarters, and reached her side. Roma turned to him with a gasp of relief, that changed to one of dismay as her eyes lit on his expression.

'I'd rather face the horses,' she thought in alarm. Earl looked infinitely more dangerous than the colts. One glance at his face was enough to tell her that he was furiously angry. He sucked in a deep, hissing breath, and his eyes glinted like bronze flints.

'No wonder,' he snapped, and grabbed her without warning round her waist. 'Get back. *Back*, I said!' With one hand he reached up to the black's head leathers, and reinforcing the stable lad's strength he pushed the big colt back in a clatter of hooves and cleared a path for himself and Roma to the door of the loose box. With his other hand he grasped her unceremoniously, tucked her under his arm, and hauled her from out of the middle of the now wildly milling animals as if she was a sack of corn, she thought furiously. With long strides he reached the safety of the stable, and dumped her forcefully back on to her feet.

'Go straight back into the house and wash it off,' he ordered her brusquely.

'Wash what off?'

Had he gone completely mad? she wondered angrily. Her fingers came up to rub her waist. It stung with the force of his grip, but not half so badly as her pride was stung by the indignity of his method of removing her from the mêlée. A small, clear-seeing, inner eye watched again the tall, commanding figure striding to her rescue, braving the deadly hooves. . . . She shook the picture out of her mind impatiently.

'What do you think caused this sort of uproar among the colts?' he snapped at her.

'The cat frightened them, what else? It ran among them, and they started stamping and jumping about all

over the place.' What did he think caused the uproar? she
wondered angrily. He told her exactly what he thought.

'The colts aren't frightened, they're excited,' he said
abruptly, 'and it's got nothing to do with the cat. You
shouldn't have followed Satan in among the horses at the
rear end of the string. Don't you know better than to get
close to young colts after soaking yourself in perfume like
that?' he shouted at her.

'Perfume? What on earth's my perfume got to do with
it?' she cried, bewildered by his unexpected attack. The
scent was strong, much too strong, she admitted ruefully.
In her haste to get down to the stable yard in time, she
had pressed the button of the atomiser too hard, and the
warmth of her body had brought out the full strength of
the heavy aroma. It hung about her person in an exotic
cloud of sweetness that wrinkled her own nose with distaste, and for some unexplained reason it seemed to act
like a red rag to a bull so far as Earl was concerned.

'It didn't upset Arabian Minty, I patted him when I
walked by, and he stood perfectly still. And my perfume's
never bothered the horses I've ridden in the past,' she
finished defiantly.

'Arabian Minty's a gelding,' Earl retorted curtly. 'And
I suppose the horses you've ridden in the past,' he
repeated her words with sarcastic inflection, 'I suppose
they've been riding stable hacks?'

'What if they have?' she flashed back, incensed by his
superior attitude. The riding stable horses might not be of
the same quality as the string that occupied his stable
yard, but they had better manners than the thoroughbreds, she told herself critically.

'Thoroughbreds aren't like ordinary hacks,' he interrupted her impatiently. 'They're finely bred, and highly
strung because of it, and it makes their reactions hair-
triggered, and sometimes violent. And for that reason they
can be dangerous.'

'I still don't see why my perfume should upset the colts,'
Roma argued stubbornly. She did *not* see why, but a quick
peep through the stable door forced her to the conclusion

that there must be something behind what the trainer said, because the bunch of colts at the rear of the string, although still frisky enough, had quietened considerably, and the stable lads were mounting, and in control again, and even as she watched, the string, led by the fillies with Cloud at the head under the guiding hand of Steve, started out from the stable yard on their morning exercise.

'If you don't see why, then I'll enlighten you,' Earl told her grimly, and did so. Tersely, baldly, in one short illuminating sentence, he enlightened her, and Roma's face flamed.

'I didn't know . . . I'd no idea. . . .' she stammered, appalled.

'Where did you imagine musk was obtained from? Daisy chains?' he enquired bitingly. 'It's used in most of the expensive perfumes, and one whiff of it's enough to make any excitable young colt well nigh unmanageable,' he drove his point home remorselessly.

'I didn't know perfumes had an animal based ingredient,' Roma denied hotly. 'Why should I? I don't dissect the make-up of every perfume I use, before I put it on.'

'Not all perfumes use musk. Some use purely floral essences, so I suggest you do a bit of research into the subject if you intend to remain in the racing world,' he retorted. 'And in the meantime,' he ordered her curtly, 'keep away from the colts, whether you're wearing perfume or not. I don't want to be responsible for you getting kicked while you're on my premises.'

Implying that it was a matter of complete indifference to him what happened to her, so long as it did not happen while she was on his property.

'I'll be able to leave your premises the very moment the Lodge is made ready for me to occupy,' she goaded him angrily. 'When I'm living in my own home,' she rubbed in her ownership deliberately, provocatively, 'I can wear what perfume I please!' She would never wear this particular perfume again, she thought shudderingly. The very presence of it on her skin made her feel unclean, now that she had been made aware of what ingredient it contained. 'I'll get some of the other sort, made purely from flowers,' she promised herself. 'I'll resort to the old-fashioned lavender bags, rather than use this type of perfume again.' But she would not let Earl know how she felt. She would not let him think he could dictate to her in such an autocratic manner.

'Since the basic idea of perfume is to attract, there won't be much point in you wearing it when you're living on your own,' he taunted her.

'I didn't wear it for your benefit, if that's what you're thinking,' she flared. 'The conceit of the man!' she thought furiously. She had used it . . . why had she used it? To boost her confidence as an armour *against* Earl, not to attract him, she reminded herself staunchly. But deep down, the question remained at the back of her mind, floating wraithlike, like the perfume itself, uneasy, unanswered.

'Since you *are* wearing it, it seems a pity to waste it.'

He caught her off guard. His hands reached out, grasping her shoulders and pulling her to him. Dimly she was aware of the last of the string of horses passing the loose box window, leaving the stable yard. Of feeling thankful that there was none of the stable staff left to see. She had time to think, 'The perfume's affected Earl, as well as his horses,' and knew that it had not. Knew that he mocked her with it, using it as an excuse to discomfit her.

'I wish I'd never put it on,' she thought in panic, and then felt traitorously glad that she had.

The touch of his lips set her on fire. They burned through her mind, confusing her thoughts. They seared her heart, so that it melted under the flame of his anger, unable to sustain her own anger against him. She tried to push him away, to free herself before her weakness overwhelmed her, but his arms held her like a vice, keeping her fast, and she could not move. His lips wandered on, exploring the long slender column of her throat, unerringly followed the line of the perfume spray. She drew in a deep, sobbing breath. She could not fight him, she told herself despairingly, because in doing so she was fighting herself, and it was tearing her in two. With a tiny moan of surrender she gave herself up to his arms.

'Earl. . . .' Her voice came out in a broken whisper.

'Go back to your airline, and the world you know,' he said harshly, and pushed her away from him, roughly, with hard hands. 'You're safe there, where you belong.'

And here she was not safe? Here, in Earl's world, she did not belong? She caught back a sob, pressing the sound back into her aching throat with desperate finger tips against her bruised and trembling lips. By his every word, every gesture, from the first moment they met, Earl had made it plain that he did not want her at Burdon Court.

'He shouldn't use a kiss like that,' her heart cried out in passionate protest. He had turned his kiss into a lash, with which to drive her away, and she raised her face, chalk white, to his, and looked out from eyes that burned dark with pain.

'Mr Paget! There's a phone call for you, Guv'nor.'

The clatter of a bucket, the slap of water from a hose-pipe, and the sound of a hard-bristled broom being wielded with cheerful vigour, proclaimed the voice to be that of the yard man. 'Phone call for you, Guv'nor,' he called again, and now Roma could hear the insistent summons of the bell from the direction of the yard office.

With a final, piercing look which seemed to spear right through her, Earl spun on his heel and strode out of the stable door. His footsteps sounded crisp and sharp on the cobbles of the yard outside, and she heard the office door open, and then slam decisively behind him, shutting him away from her. Shutting her out. She leaned trembling against the wall of the loosebox, and her brimming eyes dropped slow tears to scald her bloodless cheeks.

'California, here I come. . . .'

The yard man serenaded his way untunefully along the line of stable doors, and Roma shrank back farther into the dim recesses of the loosebox, out of sight. As soon as he had gone, she could make her escape to the sanctuary of her own room, there to face with whatever courage her failing heart could muster, the knowledge that the kisses Earl had used to drive her away, had perversely bound her to him in a bondage that, however hard she fought against it, she knew with the knowledge of despair would hold her enslaved for the rest of her days.

The whistling grew fainter, and faded away round the end of the stable block, and Roma pushed herself away from the wall, forcing her feet to hold her. It seemed to require an immense effort, but somehow she managed it, and stumbled towards the door. Soon the phone call must end, and Earl would replace the receiver and emerge from the office. Panic gripped her at the possibility that he might come back and find her still in the stable. Perhaps he might think she was waiting for him to return. . . . The thought put fresh life into her shaking limbs, and she hurried outside. The errand she came on to the stable yard would have to wait. What matter now if the newspaper photograph *was* pinned up in the stable office? People, and that included Earl, must make what they wanted of its message. So far as she herself was concerned, Roma thought bitterly, if she had any doubts before, she had none at all left now. She knew, with a sense of awful finality, that the camera had not lied.

CHAPTER THREE

'THE contractor's just telephoned, Mr Paget. He said he'd meet you at the Lodge in twenty minutes' time, if that's all right with you?'

'The Lodge?' Roma abandoned her pretence at eating her unwanted apple pie. The fluffy pastry and sweet-sharp filling was choking her in any case, she decided, and pushed her plate aside.

'He's come along to sort out what's needing to be done,' Mrs Murray told her. 'It'll be nice to see the place properly thatched and occupied again,' she added happily.

'Tell him I'll be there,' Earl cut her short as he drained his coffee cup and rose to his feet.

'I'll come with you,' Roma said determinedly. She rose too, glad to leave the table. Lunch had been a fraught meal. She could not ever remember enduring a worse, she thought bleakly. Even Mrs Murray's superb cooking could not ease the brittle tension that lay between herself and her host, and the silence that seemed to stretch for ever, broken only by brief requests to, 'Pass the salt, please,' and, 'Water? Yes, another glass full.' Salt that had not the power to bring savour to food that tasted like dust and ashes in her mouth, and could only be swallowed with the aid of copious draughts of water, so that in the end she gave up trying to eat, and remained miserably silent, the greater part of her lunch untouched.

The atmosphere did not seem to affect Earl's appetite, she thought sourly. He ate with the concentration of a hungry man who had been hard at work outdoors since dawn. She came to the table with palpitating reluctance, unwilling to stay away and admit her lack of courage; dreading to appear in case he should bring up the episode in the stable yard. His reaction was the same as that he ascribed to the thoroughbreds, she remembered ruefully; it was hair-triggered, and for that reason, dangerous. The trainer had proved deadly dangerous to her peace of mind. He had cleared the weak hurdles of her defences with humiliating ease, and romped home an easy winner, virtually unchallenged. Then, having won, he spurned the prize as not being worth the race.

The knowledge rasped her pride, bringing back hot anger to armour her against her own weak emotions. It bolstered her will to fight for her right to the Lodge, to have her say in the manner in which it should be restored. Earl should not be allowed to have all his own way, she told herself firmly.

'I'll come with you.' She did not wait to ask for his permission, she followed him out of doors and hurried

beside him towards the Land Rover. He did not attempt
to slacken his long strides, and she had to run to keep up,
but somehow she forced her legs to keep pace with him,
all the while hating him for his easy ascendancy over her,
his sheer male dominance that said without words that he
could easily outdistance her if he felt so inclined. She was
out of breath, as much with fury as with the fast pace, by
the time they reached the Land Rover. Earl opened the
door on the driving side and Roma slipped quickly round
the bonnet.

'He can't start it while I'm in front,' she told herself
breathlessly, and reached out for the door handle on the
passenger side before he could start the engine and go
without her. Even as her hand grasped the cold metal
handle, she wondered,

'What if the door's locked on this side?'

Perhaps Earl knew it was locked, and intended to let
her struggle with it, knowing her efforts would be fruitless,
and he could start the engine and drive off without her,
once again the victor in their constant battle of wills. The
thought added impetus to her strength, and she grasped
the handle and twisted it furiously, and felt almost surprised when the door opened on smooth hinges, so much
so that she staggered backwards, momentarily off balance.
With an immense effort she pulled herself together and
clambered up into the high vehicle, slammed the door
behind her, and flopped back into the seat, triumphant
and breathless as Earl started the engine and let the
vehicle forward in a silence as potent as that at the lunchtime table. But now she had something to occupy her
mind, the coming discussion with the contractor, in which
she was determined to make her wishes known.

'I've had a good look round, Mr Paget, and the structure's as sound as a bell.' The blue-overalled figure met
them on the weed-strewn front path to the Lodge, and
Roma heaved a small sigh of relief at his words. To her
untutored eyes the cottage looked virtually derelict, and
the roof as if it would never work again.

'The thatch'll have to come off, of course,' the contractor seemed quite undisturbed by the prospect, 'but the timbers underneath are as solid as a rock. They're hand-hewn oak, the same as in the Court itself, and it'll take more than weather to disturb them. It's only a matter of the covering.' He pointed upwards at the holed and rotting thatch, and Roma felt a moment's swift thankfulness that she was not the unlucky thatcher. He would need nerves of steel, she decided with a shiver, to withstand the army of creepy-crawlies that must have made the roof covering their home since the house was last occupied. 'It's just a case of whether you want straw or reed,' the man asked casually.

'Reed,' Earl said, without hesitation, and without even a glance in her direction to see if she agreed, Roma noticed angrily.

'Straw,' she instantly contradicted him. She could not see what difference it made, so long as it was thatch, she thought mutinously. She had not even realised that there *was* a choice of materials. Thatch, until now, had been to her just thatch. 'I've a right to have what covering I like on my own house,' she turned hard eyes on Earl, determined not to give way, determined to make the trainer, and the contractor, acknowledge her right as owner.

'It's up to you, miss,' the contractor said. His tone expressed doubt, and Roma's heart sank as the man's expression told her that she had made yet another faux pas, and once again displayed ignorance in front of Earl, when it was most important to her that she should appear knowledgeable and sure of herself.

'The trouble with straw——' the man tipped his cap backwards and scratched his head reflectively, and Roma bit her lip and steeled herself to listen. She refused to look at Earl. No doubt if she did, he would meet her look with an 'I told you so,' expression, she thought vexedly, and refused to give him that satisfaction. She kept her eyes steadfastly on the contractor's face. 'The trouble with straw is, it's hard to get nowadays,' the man told her regretfully. 'It'll mean waiting a goodish while, I reckon, while I try to get hold of a supply for you.'

'There's bales of the stuff at the stables,' Roma began indignantly. Really, what next excuse would workmen find not to complete a job! 'There's enough to complete a dozen roofs, let alone one,' she exaggerated. She had found the man's supply for him, and she waited with set lips for Earl to refuse to allow her to use it. 'If he says no, I'll explode!' she promised herself furiously.

'You can't use the stable straw.' The refusal came as she had predicted to herself it would, and she spun to face the trainer, her eyes flashing.

'You can't possibly need a whole barn full of the stuff,' she cried angrily. 'Why, I heard Steve say only this morning that you were thinking of clearing the last of the old straw out to make room for the fresh supply. You're just using it as an excuse to be obstructive,' she accused him bitterly.

'Stable straw isn't of any use,' Earl began, and she interrupted him hotly.

'How do you know, until it's been tried? You haven't even. . . .'

'Because it isn't long enough, miss.' The contractor took a hand and checked her furious retort in mid-stream. 'The straw for bedding down is small stuff, it's no good for thatching.'

'Surely there never used to be this difficulty over finding straw?' she questioned disbelievingly. Even the contractor seemed to be on Earl's side.

'There wasn't, until they started using combines for harvesting,' the man replied regretfully. 'The old method of reaping used to leave nice long straw that could be put to good use. It's the combines,' he explained seriously. 'They spew out the grain at one end like iron filings in a factory, and leave behind them straw that's not fit for anything but setting fire to. No, if you want straw thatch, I'll have to set about finding a supply that's been hand-gathered. It'll be costly,' he warned, and added lugubriously, 'even if I can manage to get it.' He did not sound at all sure that he could, Roma thought uneasily.

'It'll have to be reed.' Earl spoke decisively, terminating

the argument. His tone said it had gone on for quite long enough, and that he had allowed it to continue only in order to show her that she was in the wrong. Now she had learned her lesson, his expression said, he was not prepared to waste any more time arguing about something which he had already decided should be done his way, and no other. As if to emphasise his point, he glanced at his watch with ostentatious impatience.

'Reed is best, miss,' the contractor rubbed in Earl's victory with unconscious vigour. 'Good Norfolk reed in prime condition will give a lifetime's wear. You'd best forget the straw,' he advised.

She would like nothing better than to forget her whole disastrous inheritance, Roma thought balefully. 'Do whatever you think is best,' she told him shortly, and added, 'I'm going to have a look round my future home.' She lost no opportunity of emphasising her ownership, and without looking at Earl to see how he reacted, she turned her back on the two men and set off along the crazy paving path that looked as if it might do a complete circuit of the Lodge, and return to the main path leading from the gate to the front door.

'Watch yourself on the path, miss, it's a bit uneven.'

'I'll be careful,' she promised, and smiled back at the contractor, warmed by his consideration. Earl had shown no such concern.

'It needs a lot of work to put it to rights,' she murmured dubiously. She rubbed a clear space on a cracked windowpane, and surveyed the cobwebby interior with a deepening sense of depression. Until the Lodge was finished, she had no option but to remain under Earl's roof, a position which for reasons she would rather not think about, she found increasingly untenable.

'I won't leave the Court until I take possession here.' Resolutely she recharged her flagging spirits. 'If I go away and leave Earl with a clear field, there's no knowing what he'll do.' Unconsciously she found herself using racing terminology already, and she bit her tongue in vexation.

'How long . . .?' She used it out loud to better effect, as

footsteps sounded on the path just behind her, and turned with a frown when she discovered it was Earl and not the contractor who approached her.

'Eight or ten weeks, if the weather holds,' the trainer responded casually.

'I don't believe it!' She stared at him, stunned. 'It can't possibly take ten whole weeks to repair a cottage as small as this. Why, at that rate it'll be Christmas before. . . .' She choked to a halt, mounting anger stopping the words in her throat.

'It's Earl's fault,' she told herself stormily. 'He's deliberately delaying the repairs, hoping to wear me down. Hoping to make me sell him the cottage.' He was probably, she realised with a flash of insight, relying on the fact that the airline would not grant her indefinite leave of absence, hoping that she would be forced to go back to her job and leave him in sole and undisputed charge. She eyed him suspiciously. Perhaps he planned to have the repairs completed more quickly than he had suggested, so that he could move one of his staff into the Lodge while she, Roma, was safely out of the way, and then dispute her right to remove the occupant. She had heard of such things happening. . . .

'It'll be Easter before it's finished, if you insist on having straw thatch,' he pointed out slyly, and Roma's lips tightened.

'I left it to the contractor to do what he thinks fit.' She retained the reins of control firmly in her own hands. 'It's up to him, now.'

She became aware, suddenly, that she no longer had Earl's full attention. 'You might at least listen to what I have to say,' she cried, furious at being ignored, and gasped as the trainer spun on his heel and strode off along the path. Angrily, she hurried to catch up with him. 'Where . . .?'

'I'm going to remove a small boy from that apple tree, before he falls out of it,' Earl stopped just long enough to tell her, and Roma skidded to an undignified halt, taken unawares by his unscheduled stop, and in imminent danger of colliding with him in her haste to catch up.

'What boy?' It was just another excuse, she thought angrily, and then Earl raised his hand and pointed.

'The one helping himself to apples in the kitchen garden.'

She saw him then, a preoccupied small figure in jeans and jersey, half hidden in the covering of leaves that because of the mild autumn still clothed the branches. No doubt the young trespasser would have remained undiscovered but for her impromptu tour of inspection, she thought sympathetically.

'Leave him alone, he isn't doing any harm.'

The boy heard her. She intended him to. She raised her voice deliberately in order to warn him. If he was quick, she thought hopefully, he could slide down the tree on to the ground, and be out of reach before Earl got near him. There was an overgrown flower border and rickety fence between where they stood, and the kitchen garden.

In two long strides, Earl jumped the one and vaulted the other with contemptuous ease, and gained the grass under the apple tree seconds before the boy scrambled to the ground. The youthful climber landed in a rush and jumped to his feet to run, but Earl was too quick for him.

'Empty your pockets,' he commanded, and grasping the boy's jersey he helped in the process with a quick shake. The spoils of the lad's raid, half a dozen nondescript apples, tumbled out on to the grass, a green accusation at his feet.

'I only scrumped a few. The Lodge is empty. No one else wants them,' the boy pleaded his case, and Roma's heart melted at the sight of the young, freckled face and tousled red hair, looks that would be enough to make her forgive him practically anything, she thought with an indulgent smile.

'Scrumping is stealing. The apples aren't yours to take.' To Roma's amazement, Earl's stern features did not relax one iota. 'If I catch you here again I'll give you the tanning you deserve, and then march you straight to the

police station,' he threatened with a ferocious scowl that
widened the boy's eyes into saucers. 'Now cut along home,
and don't come here again,' he growled. The lad needed
no second bidding. He took to his heels, only waiting long
enough to shout back in childish defiance when he knew
himself to be safely out of reach,

'I'll get me own back, I will!' before he disappeared
from sight round a corner of the hedge.

'Did you have to scare the wits out of the child?' Roma
reached the sagging fence and gripped the top rail with
angry fingers. 'The apples can't be of any use to you,
they're only scrubby little things, not fit to use.' She made
a mental note to have the tree pruned when she moved
into the Lodge. Her move there would improve the
quality of the fruit, as well as of her own life style, she
thought bitingly.

'They're only small fruit, but they're sweet, more's the
pity.' Earl picked up two of the larger ones from the pitiful
little pile on the ground. 'If they didn't taste good, they
wouldn't be attractive to the children. I'd rather scare
them away than risk one of them falling out of the tree
and getting hurt. Try Silver Cloud with one,' he suggested, and tossed the two apples to her. 'The filly won't
refuse it. She's like all her sex for enjoying forbidden fruit,'
he jibed.

'You. . . .' His grin stung her to furious action.
Automatically she fielded the fruit as it arced towards
her, and then impulsively she drew her arm back, the first
apple grasped tightly in her hand.

'Don't,' Earl warned her quickly.

She did. The apple left her fingers before the ominous
note in his voice had time to register. Roma had been
brought up with cricketing brothers, and her aim was
straight and true. The apple flew through the air like a
hard green bullet, straight at Earl's head. He ducked in
the nick of time, and it flew over him, and landed harm-
lessly in the bushes behind him. Roma was gripped by an
almost irresistible desire to giggle. It evaporated with the
same speed as her missile as she caught sight of the ex-

pression on the trainer's face.

She could not run. She had picked her way across a tangled border to reach the fence, and a pencil-slim skirt and court shoes did not allow her the freedom to jump back over the briars the same as Earl had done. They barred her way, clung to her clothing, tripped her so that her feet stumbled. She regained her balance, and looked wildly round her for a way of escape.

'I'll make you pay for that!'

He was as good as his word. She fought, but he was stronger than she was, and overpowered her struggles with ease. He gripped her wrists with fingers that felt like bands of steel, and forced her hands behind her back as he put his arms right round her, bending her backwards so that her face was upturned to his. The second apple dropped unheeded from her nerveless fingers as his lips punished her for throwing the first one at him. She tried to turn her face away, but the hot anger of his kiss forced her head back like a slender reed bent helplessly before the fury of a storm. It drove her lips against her teeth, bruising, hurting. She tried to cry out in protest, but the only sound that emerged was a whimper, and that, too, trailed into silence.

Flip Dean's kisses had been lingering, sensuous, extracting the last ounce of enjoyment from each caress. Earl's kiss was hard, demanding, and angry. An insult! Roma told herself furiously, the more angry because she discovered she was fighting herself even harder than she was trying to fight Earl.

Vaguely she was aware of the faint smell of good aftershave lotion, the clean smell of tweed. His arms were hard around her, his closeness enveloped her. After an endless, breathless, subduing age, his lips travelled on, seeking the crease in her cheek that was a dimple when she smiled. They traced the delicate line of her jaw, drawing a low murmur from her lips until they returned there to still it, turning his punishment into rapture—a sweet, wanton rapture, that flooded over her, taking command of her, so that it sapped her strength, until at last she ceased to fight him, and with a sigh of surrender she gave herself up to his arms. A dangerous rapture, that undermined her will and brought to the surface all the treacherous, unwanted emotions that the newspaper photograph had so cruelly revealed, and which she would fain have kept hidden, even from herself.

'That's only a foretaste of what will happen, if you dare to throw anything at me again,' he grated, and thrust her away from him.

'But . . . I. . . .' She stared up at him, dazed, and the rapture faded like the afterglow of sunset, its illusory warmth meeting the darkness of harsh reality in his set face, his hard eyes, and the cynical contempt of his expression. He loosed her arms, and she rubbed her wrists, reddened and tingling where his fingers had gripped them.

'So think before you try it again,' he warned her harshly.

'I hate you!' she breathed, through lips that were still numb from his kisses. Fierce rage rose within her. 'How could I be so gullible?' she stormed at herself. Earl used his kisses to lash her, to punish her, but she would show him he could not curb her spirit in that way.

'I hate you!' She raised her hand to strike him, but the blow did not have time to land. He caught her wrist with a quickly raised hand, and his fingers closed round it again, harder than before, with a bone-crushing force that made her wince, would have made her cry out, but pride forced the cry back, though her teeth dug into her lower lip with a force that made the blood flow. It tasted salty against her tongue, and the shock of it stung her into furious retaliation. She flung her arm upwards to try to break his hold—futilely, since he held her easily, without effort.

'You can't break me, like you break in your yearlings,' she panted defiantly. 'Use your curbs on your horses. They don't work on human beings.' She flung away from him, forgetting that he still held her, and found herself brought up short by his hold upon her wrist. He loosed it, but only to reach out and grasp her by the shoulders, not giving her time to escape. He pulled her back to face him, roughly, as if he found the urge to shake her almost irresistible.

'It's high time somebody curbed you,' he growled savagely, and Roma caught her breath, her defiance wilting in the face of his furious glare.

It told her, in no uncertain terms, that the somebody would be himself. And if any hand was to be applied to the curb, he intended it to be his own.

CHAPTER FOUR

'It's a cruel thing, to have to watch you three tucking into Mrs Murray's pie, and me having to make do on food fit only for a rabbit,' Mick mourned.

'When you retire from riding horses, and take up training them, you can eat whatever you like,' Earl replied unsympathetically from the head of the table.

'I wouldn't make a good trainer, I couldn't stand the owners,' the jockey confessed. 'I get along fine with the horses, but the owners. . . .' He shook his head sadly and crunched through his plate of salad with an air of resignation. 'Present company excepted, of course,' he grinned across the table at Roma, asking forgiveness.

'It's a shame,' she sympathised, smiling back at him, ready to forgive him anything for being friendly. It made a pleasant contrast to Earl.

'Mick mustn't put on an ounce of weight before we go to Auteuil,' Steve, the head lad, took Earl's part. 'The French races are real fast. Their hurdles are only there for show, in comparison with ours, and the pace is something to watch,' he said enthusiastically. 'The whole field end up running for their lives, off the bit.' His description did not seem to call for any comment, which was just as well, Roma thought amusedly, for she had long ago got lost in his technicalities. 'The two horses have already gone,' Steve returned to the realms of understandable conversation, 'they need twenty-four hours to settle down before a race.'

'Which ones have you sent?' Roma was not really interested, but pride forced her to ask, to keep up her end of the conversation in front of Earl. She had answered the summons of the dinner gong with heart-thumping trepidation, dreading having to face the trainer again, but refusing to remain upstairs and eat her dinner in solitude, and thus admit defeat, although her courage quailed at the prospect of sitting through another solitary meal with her host. A wave of relief flooded over her when the jockey and the head lad put in an appearance at the table, even though the talk between the men was all of racing. Earl could not even allow them to eat their meals in peace, she thought critically, purposely blinding herself to the fact that it was probably the reason why they had been invited to dinner with the trainer in the first place.

'Arabian Minty and Silver Cloud,' Steve answered her question laconically, and Roma's head came up with a quick jerk. So her own horse and Earl's were to be rivals in the same race? They would have competed before, if Earl had not scratched the grey at the last moment. Would he use the same excuse, and withdraw her filly this time? Was he afraid that Silver Cloud might beat Arabian Minty to the post? Deliberately she looked straight at Earl, her eyes challenging him, and received her answer in his return stare.

No, he was not afraid. His silent, steely regard told her that there were few things capable of making Earl Paget feel afraid. And yes, his look said, if the conditions were right, both the horses would run. And there was something else, something unfathomable in his eyes, that puzzled her. A look as of some secret knowledge, that she did not share. It made her feel faintly uneasy. She bit her lip, and hastily let it go again; it was still sore from where she had bitten it before. Pride would not allow her to ask questions of either Earl or his staff, and she relapsed into silence, her mind darting here and there, wondering, probing, thinking of a dozen possibilities, and rejecting them all.

'Will you be coming to Auteuil with us, Miss Roma?' Steve broke into her preoccupation with a question, and Roma looked at him vaguely, her mind not registering for the moment what he had said. 'Silver Cloud's pacing, but you'll like the sport there,' he assured her, misunderstanding her silence, 'it's a fashionable course.'

'We're going to France to race horses, not to look at fashions,' Earl cut in repressively, and Roma threw him a glance of pure dislike. It was almost like being on a seesaw, she thought without humour. One moment she was responding to him, and the next she detested him. It was much easier when she detested him.

'I'll come, of course,' she replied instantly, without waiting to see if Earl would second the invitation. She knew that he would not. 'As Silver Cloud's owner, I've got every right to go and watch my own horse race,' she told herself mutinously.

'There isn't time to renew your passport,' Earl said curtly. 'We're flying out tomorrow.' His tone said he hoped her passport was no longer valid.

'As I'm an air hostess, my passport's always valid,' Roma thrust back swiftly.

Earl did not know that she was no longer an air hostess, and for excellent reasons she had no intention of telling him, she thought angrily. Let the lie serve her purpose. She let it rest uncorrected between them without compunction.

'I suggest you look to your own passport. And the horse's, if necessary,' she added with heavy sarcasm.

'My own passport's just been renewed,' Earl replied levelly, 'and,' he paused, and the glint in his eyes warned Roma of the coup de grâce to come, 'and since it's the first time the horse has travelled abroad, Silver Cloud's passport is brand new.'

'How was I to know that a horse needed a passport?' Roma asked herself crossly the next morning, dropping necessities for the journey haphazardly into her shoulder bag in preparation for an early start. Once again Earl had gained the upper hand, she thought discontentedly, and the amusement of Mick and Steve, kindly though it had been, still rankled.

'Earl only wins because he knows more about racing than I do. On the flight to France I'll be back in the world I know, and that should even the score in my favour, at least for a while,' she comforted herself. She closed the zip on her bag with a quick tug, and ran downstairs to join the three men in a more cheerful frame of mind.

'With a bit of luck I'll find a seat on my own, or maybe sit with Steve on the plane,' she hoped as Earl put herself and the head lad into the back seat of the car with a quick order to Mick to ride in the front with him, when the jockey was about to follow them.

'I want to talk to you about the race.'

She did not want to sit in the front with Earl, but illogically she resented being banished to the back seat with the head lad. She would have liked to have a choice. It would have given her an opportunity to refuse Earl.

The trainer ignored her presence, and concentrated on talking racing tactics to Mick. Steve did not seem to mind, he did not seem to expect anything else, but Roma sat and simmered in silent resentment, even though she had not enough knowledge of racing to join in the conversation. But she could listen, and learn, she told herself. There was little else she could do, in the closed vehicle, she thought crossly.

'Hold him up until the last bend, then let him go,' Earl instructed the jockey. 'Keep him from hugging the fence. . . .'

It was strange how everyone called horses 'he', Roma mused. Silver Cloud was a filly, a 'she'.

'Don't let him have his head, or he'll pull your arms off.'

'I won't,' the jockey promised cheerfully. 'Minty and me, we've got an understanding between us,' he grinned.

'I thought you were riding Silver Cloud?' Somehow she

had taken it for granted that Mick would be riding her own horse. It came as a distinct shock to learn that he was not, that he was to ride Earl's horse instead. Logic told her that the jockey could not ride both the horses in the same race, but. . . .

'Bob's riding Cloud,' Mick spoke to her over his shoulder, matter-of-factly. Bob was the stable lad who looked after Cloud and Minty, she knew. He was an apprentice jockey, a young lad still gaining experience, about to ride her horse against Mick who was already a veteran of the courses.

'Bob won't have a chance against Mick!' Roma's anger spilled over. It meant Silver Cloud would not have a chance against Minty. 'Earl's determined not to let my horse win,' she fumed silently. That must have been the knowledge she saw in his eyes at the dinner table last night, the secret knowledge that she, in her ingorance, could not share. Earl had already made certain that her horse had not got a chance against his own. 'What hope has an apprentice jockey got against a professional of Mick's standing?' she cried hotly. 'What can Bob do? You might just as well scratch Cloud from this race as well,' she declared bitterly.

'Bob will ride to my instructions, or I'll want to know the reason why,' Earl retorted sharply.

'And what are your instructions to Bob?' she demanded. 'To lose the race, I suppose,' she answered herself before he could speak. 'To stay behind, so that your horse can take the prize!'

She registered the surprise on the faces of the jockey and the head lad even as she heard Earl's indrawn breath, sharp and clear like the hiss of a snake in the confines of the car. He turned round slowly in his seat and faced her. The car stopped, and her own heart seemed to stop with it. Earl looked at her, his glare transfixed her, it seemed to bore a hole right through her, through which her own breath fled, and her courage followed it. She quailed before the primitive anger that blazed in his eyes. She had accused him of malpractice, questioned his professional integrity, and therefore his pride, and what was worse, she had questioned it in front of the men in his employ.

'We're blocking the pull-in, Guv'nor. We're causing a traffic jam,' Mick intervened hurriedly, and Roma became conscious of a cacophony of hooting horns behind them, indignantly demanding to know why they should stop in such a traffic-blocking spot. She became aware of the dark rise of bricks and mortar outside the car windows. It was the terminal building. They had reached the airport.

'You'll have to move on, Guv'nor,' Mick pleaded. 'You're attracting the attention of the airport police.'

Earl moved. With a final, gimlet glare that warned Roma that so far as he was concerned the matter was only shelved, and not forgotten, he turned and put the car in motion again, and the horns stopped blowing, and the angry words died on Roma's lips, because even if she could screw up the courage to utter them, there was no time now for recriminations, no time for the bitter accusations that burned on the edge of her tongue. The bustle of the airport claimed them, the familiar queue at the Customs post, the crowded scenes of greetings and fare-wells. They were carried along with it, willy-nilly. Earl left them at the terminal entrance while he parked the car, and rejoined them to shepherd them through the formalities.

'As if I don't know how to cope for myself,' Roma thought impatiently. Most of the airport staff were familiar to her, let alone the routine of the formalities. She found herself hailed by friendly voices from all sides, and when they climbed the steps into the plane, it was Jane who stood to greet them at the door.

'I couldn't believe my luck when I saw your name on the passenger list,' the air hostess enthused. 'I was only switched on to the Continental run at the last minute because the other stewardess went down with 'flu. How do you like retirement?' she asked, and her eyes slid mischievously in Earl's direction.

Did Jane *have* to use that word? Roma asked herself restlessly. She frowned, and gave her ex-colleague a warning shake of her head. Jane was prone to tease, and the trend of her thoughts was all too clear. She eyed Earl with open approval. Putting two and two together, and making five, Roma deduced tartly.

'I've got to stop her somehow,' she told herself desperately. Perhaps Earl had not noticed the significance of her choice of words, but the trainer was a shrewd man, and one more remark like that would be enough to give the game away completely. Panic built up inside her. Earl must not know she had given up her job, and with it, her income. It would give him just the opening he needed to pressurise her into selling him the Lodge, once he realised she was living on her savings. He would know she could not hold out indefinitely. Or perhaps he would simply wait, biding his time until her funds ran out, and she had no option but to let her inheritance go? Her mouth felt dry. Fervently she wished Earl fitted Jane's first, flippant description of him:

'Bandy legs, and a frightful hacking jacket.'

If he had, the air hostess would not evince the flattering interest which she accorded the trainer now. Roma turned her frown into a ferocious scowl, but she might as well have saved herself the effort, she realised despairingly, as Jane ushered them happily into the plane, and to their seats. Practically tucked them in, Roma thought impatiently, herself beside the window, and Earl in the seat next to her, hemming her in. There was little she could do about it. Short of openly refusing to sit by the trainer, and causing a public fuss, she was obliged to accept Jane's arrangement with as good a grace as she could muster.

'The very second we're aloft, I'll make an excuse and go to the ladies' room,' she determined grimly. Once on her own she would buttonhole Jane, and straighten her out. From the look on her face, the air hostess had practically got herself and Earl eloping, she thought, panic-stricken, long experience of her romantically minded colleague making her fear the worst if Jane's starry-eyed behaviour was allowed to go unchecked.

'Fasten your seat belts, please.'

The plane taxied on to the runway, and the familiar flight routine began. Jane bent to help an elderly woman passenger with her seat belt. Roma found she had to make a conscious effort to prevent herself from checking Earl's belt. It had all been a part of her life for so long, that it was difficult to realise she was no longer actively involved. She was just an ordinary passenger, a looker-on.

The plane stopped, and turned, and the pilot brought the engine up to full revs. 'To see if all the nuts and bolts are still tight,' Flip used to laughingly put it. The plane quivered like a live thing, urgent for flight, every inch of the machine protesting at being held down on the alien ground. The elderly woman passenger began to show signs of nerves, and Jane bent over her, soothing, talking. Roma could almost repeat her words, although she could not hear what Jane said. She had used the same ones herself, dozens of times.

'There's nothing to worry about. The pilot always checks to satisfy himself that everything's absolutely secure before we set off. It's a routine safety precaution, that's all.'

The pilot was evidently satisfied. The engines quietened, the plane stilled, then the roar rose again, but with a different note this time, not the frustrated noise of leashed power, but the confident surge of machinery taking the load it was designed for. The tarmac of the runway began to roll beneath them, gathering speed until it flashed past in a dark blur. The nose of the plane tilted upwards, and Roma lay back in her seat, relishing the feel of the powerful machine as it rose smoothly into its own element. Soon Jane would be coming round with coffee.

Roma kept her gaze steadfastly out of the window, away from Earl, but her eyes scarcely saw the countryside that opened up below them like a huge map. However hard she looked away, her every nerve end was conscious of him, rawly aware of him sitting beside her. What was he thinking about? Had he guessed? Did he suspect?

'Coffee?'

She jumped when he suddenly spoke to her, and checked herself sharply. If she kept on like this, she thought desperately, he would soon begin to realise that something was amiss. She had been so engrossed in her own thoughts, she had not noticed Jane coming along the gangway with a tray.

'I'll be back,' the hostess promised.

'Perhaps the pilot will keep her talking,' Roma hoped. She could do without Jane's indiscreet comments at the moment. Maybe the elderly woman would have another attack of nerves, and demand the stewardess's attention. She sipped her coffee, not because she wanted it, but because it gave her something to do. Something to fix her attention upon, and try to forget Earl sitting beside her, so close to her that she could feel the fine wool of his jacket sleeve brushing against her arm, as he raised his own coffee cup to his lips. The silence stretched between them, until her nerves twanged like fiddle strings, vibrating to his every move.

'Stop it!' she commanded herself angrily, but it was easier said than done, and she felt a surge of contrary relief when Jane appeared once more beside them.

'The Captain sends his compliments, and asks if you'd like to join him on the flight deck,' she grinned, her merry face belying her formal invitation.

Deliverance! With trembling fingers, Roma divested herself of her seat belt and stood up.

'I didn't realise we were over the Channel already.' She tried to make her voice sound normal, matter-of-fact. Tried not to let the relief show. Bless the Captain, whoever he was, she thought thankfully. She could remain on the flight deck until it was time to land, remain away from Earl. The pilot's invitation came just at the right time. It would show the trainer that somebody found her company desirable, even if he did not. She slanted a glance at his face, wondering if he had taken the point, and discovered he was looking at Jane, not herself, as the hostess went on hospitably,

'Mr Paget's included in the invitation. That is, if he's interested?'

'I am indeed.'

Earl got to his feet with alacrity, and Roma stared at him, nonplussed. His enthusiasm showed an abundance of interest, but whether it was centred in the technicalities of the flight deck, or in the air hostess herself, it was difficult to decide, she thought sourly. Unexpectedly, a flash of pure jealousy shot through her, like a red-hot knife. The shock of it stopped her in her tracks, and the pain of it made her gasp.

'I can't possibly be jealous,' she told herself, aghast. She was not of a jealous nature. She had never experienced a qualm over Flip Dean's other girl-friends. But Earl was not Flip. Earl was different. . . .

She trod the familiar way to the flight deck with her head in a whirl. She opened the door, and stepped inside, and came up behind the pilot's seat. The whirl in her head stopped with a sickening jolt as the pilot turned round and hailed her cheerily.

'Well, if it isn't my favourite girl-friend,' Flip grinned— the infectious, toothpaste advert grin that she knew so well, and that had yet never managed to unsettle the rhythm of her heart as Earl's frown was capable of doing now. 'You already know Johnny, my co-pilot,' Flip added, and waited.

'Meet Earl Paget.' She did not want to introduce him. She did not want to even acknowledge that he was there. But he stood behind her, crowding her in the confined space of the flight deck, and she had no option but to make him known to her ex-colleagues. She ground out the words through stiff lips, and hoped Flip and Johnny would not notice the tremble in her voice as she spoke his name, the tremble that betrayed a thumping heart, and shaking limbs, and all because Earl's hand touched her arm as they stood close together just inside the door. The slight contact sent a stab of pain through her like an electric shock, and for a desperate minute she feared she might faint. Then Johnny said,

'What brings you on the Paris run, Roma? Are you on holiday?' The co-pilot questioned her with the frankness of long association. Really, Roma thought, goaded into clear-headedness again by a surge of irritation, airline staff were the limit! The nature of their job turned them into a closely knit group of people, whose off-duty hours frequently had to be spent far from home, and so for the sake of companionship they were usually spent in one another's company, and it became almost impossible to keep one's private life a secret.

'We're going to Auteuil, to the races,' she replied shortly, and added, 'My horse is running.' That should put an end to the conjecture in the pilot's eyes, she thought crossly; they were both looking at Earl and herself as if they had already decided between them that the two were on honeymoon.

'What's it feel like to be among the ranks of the wealthy?' Flip teased. 'Tell me what you call your horse, and I'll put a bet on the animal the next time I'm anywhere near a racecourse,' he promised.

'Her name's Silver Cloud. And as for the bet, I shouldn't, if I were you,' Roma advised him tartly. 'I don't expect her to win.' She ignored Flip's look of surprise and added, 'Earl's the filly's trainer.' That put Earl firmly in his place, she decided with unrepentant malice. It made it look, at least on the surface, as if she employed him, and as if she was bringing him to the races in his professional capacity, rather than he bringing her as an unwelcome addition to his party. It also put the blame squarely on Earl, if Silver Cloud should lose the race. . . .

'Silver Cloud's an appropriate name for an air hostess's horse,' the co-pilot smiled, and Roma recognised the danger too late.

'Ex-air hostess, you mean,' Flip corrected him. 'The airline hasn't been the same since you left us,' he mourned.

Roma groaned. It was out, and there was nothing she could do about it. She did not dare to look at Earl. She felt him stiffen, his arm hard against her own. He knew now that she had lied to him. What was worse, she told herself worriedly, he was in a position to take advantage of his knowledge.

'Why did I have to insist on coming here with him in the first place?' she asked herself bitterly. 'Why didn't I stay at home instead?' Unconsciously she called Burdon Court 'home'. 'If I'd only stopped to think, I might have known something like this would happen. If it hadn't been Flip, it would have been someone else.' Travelling by air, it was almost inevitable, since she was known to all the airline staff.

'Look out, Paris, here we come!' Flip straightened in his seat as the dark blur on the horizon came nearer, and proclaimed its identity. 'You've got a nice day down there for your racing, Roma.' He pointed to where the capital lay sprawled in the sunshine below them. 'I wish we were coming with you,' he said enviously.

'I wish *I* was coming with *you*,' Roma echoed fervently, but she kept her wish to herself. It would only cause more comment if she voiced her discontent, and there must be enough rumours flying around the airline staff as it was, she deduced ruefully. 'It's time we went back to our seats,' she said crisply, instead, to Earl, 'we'll be landing in a few minutes.' It felt good, just for once, to be the one giving the instructions to the trainer, instead of the other way around, she told herself with satisfaction, and slipped into her place by the window as the request came over the cabin loudspeaker,

'Will all passengers please fasten their seat belts.'

And they were into the routine in reverse, touching down to a perfect landing, and waving goodbye to the crew. For a second or two, seeing Jane's familiar figure grow smaller until it disappeared, lost to sight by distance and the crowd of passengers milling around in the French terminal, Roma was gripped by a sense of desolation, and she had to give herself a mental shake and force herself to follow on behind Earl and Mick, force herself not to turn and run back to Jane and Flip and the safe, familiar world she knew. It was too late to indulge in regrets now. Too late for anything except to take her place beside Earl in the taxi he hailed for them. Mick and Steve perched on the pull-down seats opposite to them, and the jockey asked Earl interestedly,

'Did you enjoy your trip to the flight deck, Guv'nor? It's a nice change to know someone who's a V.I.P.,' he grinned engagingly at Roma.

She was not a V.I.P. any longer. She was no one special to the airline any more. No one special to Earl. The cold sense of desolation washed over her once more as Earl answered Mick,

'It was very interesting, and——' his eyes found Roma's, found and held them in a steady, level stare that told her he knew her lie had been a deliberate one, told her that he despised her for it, and intended to see that she paid the penalty for deceiving him, in a coin of his own choosing. 'I found the trip to the flight deck a very interesting one,' he said evenly, and added significantly, for Roma's benefit, 'interesting—and very enlightening.'

CHAPTER FIVE

THE racecourse was crowded.

'I told you it was a fashionable course,' Steve boasted. 'If you get bored with watching the racing, you can always look at the dresses.' His merry wink told Roma that he was not above appreciating that aspect of Auteuil himself, and she smiled back. At least Mick and Steve were friendly, she thought gratefully, and since the head lad was not riding, his company would act as a buffer between herself and Earl.

'I need a buffer of some kind,' she thought wearily. Armour plate would come in useful. Unspoken thoughts lay pregnant between herself and the trainer. Unspoken accusations, and silent defiance, and the reckoning that must surely come later, loaded the atmosphere between them like an electric storm brooding, threatening, waiting for the word, the gesture, that would unleash its pent up fury.

'Enjoy today, and never mind later,' she commanded herself robustly. 'Never mind Earl. . . .' The sunshine helped a little. Unconsciously it caused her to relax. St Luke's little summer bathed the world in a benign warmth, Nature's last kindly act before the winter storms cowed the earth into quivering submission.

Bright dresses and hats made gay splashes of colour in the well dressed crowd. Laughter, and lilting conversation, that because of her knowledge of languages did not seem strange to Roma, all combined to lift her spirits, and helped by the knowledge that her own silk suit was a perfect choice for the occasion. Softly patterned in shadows of grey, and blue, and dusky pink, it warmed her eyes, and added delicate colour to her cheeks. She knew she looked good, and the knowledge made her feel good, boosting her confidence so that to her surprise she found herself actually beginning to enjoy the novelty of her surroundings, the colourful crowd, the lovely backdrop of the surrounding countryside, and the heady, infectious excitement of the coming sport. Whether she would actually enjoy the race in which Silver Cloud and Arabian Minty were to compete was another matter.

Her stomach contracted in a tight knot as the horses lined up at the start. Cloud seemed restless, and the apprentice jockey failed twice in his attempts to mount her. Each time the grey fidgeted away, and then Earl took a hand and with a firm hold he kept the filly standing until the boy was safely aboard.

'Remember your instructions,' he told the lad.

'I will, Guv'nor.'

'Don't get any way-out ideas of your own, or you'll account for them to me.'

'I won't, Guv'nor.'

'Ride her on the bit.'

Surely the night before, at dinner, Steve had said the horses in the French races ran off the bit, not on it? Roma shrugged, and gave up the unequal attempt to cope with racing jargon.

'I will, Guv'nor.'

'Sit tight, and keep out of trouble.'

Did he have to go on at the boy so? Roma wondered irritably. Surely Bob should be encouraged to ride his best, and win, not just keep out of trouble? The apprentice jockey was probably quite nervous enough as it was, having to race against men more experienced than he was himself, without Earl nagging, and making it worse.

'Watch her, she's still restless,' Earl cautioned as he loosed the head leathers. 'If she rears and tries to flip over on her back, lean on her.'

'Why should it be Cloud who might misbehave?' Roma asked him indignantly as the grey moved off beside Arabian Minty. 'Why should you think Cloud might rear and go over, and not your horse?' He seemed to be taking every opportunity to denigrate her own filly, she thought indignantly.

'Colts don't flip over on their backs, only the fillies try that sort of nonsense,' he retorted curtly. 'They're like all the fair sex, their behaviour is unpredictable,' he added cuttingly, and turned on his heel, leaving her shaking and furious, and unable to think of a suitable answer.

'Walk on beside Mick,' Earl called his last instruction to the boy, and the chestnut and the grey moved off together. Roma frowned as she watched them go. The filly pranced, and sidestepped, and generally behaved in a restless fashion, different from the gelding, she acknowledged grudgingly. Minty strode sedately enough under Mick's guidance as they made their way towards the starting stalls.

'I thought Bob said the horses had travelled well?' she began critically, and Earl answered her before Steve could speak.

'They did, they're both in the pink of condition.'

'But Cloud. . . .' Could it be that the apprentice was not yet capable of handling the horse properly? she wondered suspiciously. Did Earl know that? And perhaps

mount him in the race for that reason, to make sure that
Cloud would not win?

'The filly's in perfect condition. She's excited, that's
all.'

'I'm not wearing perfume.' Roma's anger boiled over.
'Not that kind of perfume, anyway,' she flared. After her
experience in the stable yard, did he not think she had
more sense?

'I know.' Earl threw her a cool, amused glance, a glance
that made her want to hit him. 'The filly's nervous at the
prospect of the race, that's all. She's never been to Auteuil
before, it's all new to her.'

It was all new to Roma, but it was the trainer who
made her nervous, not the racecourse. The close, magnetic
proximity of him set her heart beating, making a racecourse of her veins as the wildly pulsing blood throbbed
in her temples like the beat of pounding hooves, until she
longed to close her palms over them for fear her head
would burst. Earl looked down at her, watching her expression, gauging her reaction to a nicety as he added,
'Minty's been racing for several years, he's an old hand at
it now, and it doesn't bother him, but the filly's just starting on her career, and she's on edge. Exactly as you would
be in your first week at a new job,' he added deliberately.

Her breath caught in her throat, and she looked up at
him, quickly, suspiciously. Was it just a casual remark?
Or was it the first salvo of a bombardment, now that he
knew she had given up her job with the airline? She
opened her mouth to retaliate, to tell him that it was not
his concern if she had given up her job, and that she had
no intention of seeking another one. To tell him she had
her own means, and would use them all, if necessary, to
keep the Lodge. Only she knew how slender those means
were. She drew in a deep breath, prepared to hurl his
words back at him.

'They're all into the stalls now.'

Steve spoke, and Earl raised his binoculars to his eyes.
Roma shut her mouth with an angry snap, the words that
spilled on the edge of her tongue unspoken. It was im-

possible, she fumed, to talk to a man who held binoculars to his eyes. It was like trying to shout at someone enclosed in a glass-walled room. She could see him, and watch every move he made, but she could not reach him.

'They're away!'

Steve leaned forward, tense with excitement. 'There's Minty, look. And Cloud!' His excitement was infectious. In spite of herself, it reached out to grip Roma, urgent, compelling. The horses bunched as they left the stalls so that it was difficult to see which was which without the aid of fieldglasses, and Roma scorned to ask to borrow Earl's.

'I'll get some of my own before the next race,' she promised herself. But good fieldglasses were expensive, and she could not afford to indulge in luxuries. She would need all her savings to enable her to keep the Lodge.

'The first fence will thin them out.'

It loomed ahead of the riders, still closely bunched as they raced round the first bend of the track. The fence did not look very high. Roma remembered Steve's description of the French hurdles:

'Visual obstacles, rather than something to jump over.'

But at the pace the horses were galloping, the hurdles did not need to be very high. Roma felt her heart contract as the leading horse rose. It cleared the hurdle and raced on, and a second horse followed. She strained her eyes to try to pick out Cloud. Somewhere in the middle of the madly racing horses, running at a speed that took her breath away, was her own horse, ridden—she swallowed painfully—ridden by an inexperienced boy.

'Don't let them fall! Please, don't let them fall. . . .' Her fingers felt as if they would crack under the pressure as she clasped her hands together against her mouth. She could not see how such a tightly packed bunch of horses, running at such a speed, could possibly remain on their feet.

'One's down!'

She gasped as Steve cried out, and felt Earl go rigid beside her. The crowd stopped their wild cheering, and a low murmur ran through the close-packed ranks of people, like a ripple of wind through standing corn. A murmur of horror.

'He took off too soon, and crashed.'

What did it matter how it happened? Roma asked herself wildly. The fact that it had happened at all was enough. The tension of the crowd changed from excitement to fear, for the horse, for the jockey—Roma could feel their fear pressing in on her, like a solid wall.

'They're riding too close. He'll bring the ones behind him down as well.'

Was Cloud one of those behind? Or Minty? Roma went cold all over. Without warning, the other side of racing was being presented to her, the other, brutal side. As well as excitement and triumph, there lurked danger and disaster.

'Another one's down . . . no, he's not, he's only pecked. He's running on.'

'Which one is it?' Roma begged. 'I can't see.' She could not see for the rush of tears that blurred her eyes. She brushed her hand across them, and when her vision cleared she could not credit what she saw.

'The other horses are still running. Why don't they stop the race, and go back to see . . .?' She dared not voice what she thought they might see, if they went back.

'They're in the race to ride, not to go into reverse,' Earl cut short her anxious cry, and she stared up at him, stunned.

'How can you be so callous?' she cried angrily. Her voice came out in a strangled accusation, shocked, disbelieving, trying hard not to believe. 'How can you?' A sob tore at her throat, a thin thread of hysteria rising the note at the end.

'They're going too fast to stop,' Earl retorted impatiently. 'If the ones in the front turned, those at the back would just pile into them, and the result would be chaos. Someone might easily get killed.'

'What do you imagine has happened to the jockey who fell?' Roma demanded hotly.

'If he's got any sense, he's rolled out of the way and covered his head until the field are gone by and he can safely get to his feet,' Earl retorted crisply.

'He's already on his feet, Guv'nor. Look, he's walking away to the side of the track—he's not been hurt,' Steve butted in, and Roma felt herself go weak with relief. The last of the horses raced on, and she watched the small figure in the bright silks with incredulous eyes as he walked disconsolately off the course. 'His horse has carried on,' Steve unwittingly removed her next concern.

'Loose horses are a menace.' The mutter came from Earl, and he raised his glasses to his eyes again, contemptuously dismissing her layman's fears, Roma thought, incensed.

'Can't someone catch it?' she asked, instinctively.

It was a silly question, she knew that even as she asked it, but it was a very natural one.

'How?' Earl asked drily, without removing his binoculars from his eyes, and Roma felt her face go hot.

'The man's impossible!' she told herself wrathfully. Anyone else would have laughed with her, made a kindly joke of her naïveté, but Earl did not even attempt to be civil.

'There'll be another crash at the next fence if they don't get rid of the loose one,' Steve predicted, and Roma followed his gaze to where the riderless animal careered along with the others, unchecked now its jockey was no longer aboard. The field was spread out now, the pace was beginning to tell and the less able contestants to lag behind, and it was possible to see and recognise each individual animal. The loose horse was like a rudderless ship, Roma saw worriedly. It veered from side to side of the track, causing the other contestants to swerve and jostle, reducing their speed and spoiling their chances.

'It's running up beside Cloud,' Steve muttered, and Roma felt a cold, hard lump form in her stomach, tightening her nerves until she could have screamed aloud with the tension.

'Let her out, boy! Let her out!' Earl muttered aloud.

Her? He must mean Cloud. He called Minty 'him'. Roma stared at the trainer, astonished. Earl was the last person she would expect to urge on the grey. Urge on her horse, not his own.

'Let her . . . ah, good lad!'

Earlier, Roma would have declared it impossible, so fast was the pace already, but Silver Cloud lengthened her stride and ran clear of the loose horse, racing out in front of the field like a silver streak, and leaving the rest of the contestants behind her.

'Cloud! Come on, Cloud!'

A shout of unrestrained jubilation rose to Roma's lips. Steve looked at her, she thought oddly, but she did not care. Perhaps he was surprised to discover a normally quiet, restrained girl giving way to her feelings in such an uninhibited fashion, she thought amusedly, and she did not care about that, either. Cloud was out in front of the field, and running for her life, albeit in a controlled fashion. Even her uninitiated eyes could appreciate that the apprentice jockey had his mount supremely well controlled. He rode easily, confidently. And he led the field! A bunch of other horses sat in behind, Roma noticed Arabian Minty was one, keeping station as if they were unable or unwilling to make the extra effort to break out and challenge the grey for the lead. She clapped her hands delightedly.

'I can't believe it?' she gasped. 'Cloud's going to win!' In spite of Earl, her horse led the field. Nothing could prevent her from winning now, she thought exultantly.

'It's a good way to the post yet,' Steve warned, unmoved by her jubilation, and Roma stared at him, taken aback.

'He's as bad as Earl,' she told herself disgustedly. She viewed the two professionals with puzzled eyes. The entire crowd of racegoers was going wild with excitement, and her two companions remained seemingly untouched by it all. She could understand Earl not shouting for her own horse, she thought bitterly, but at least the head lad might share in her enthusiasm. 'If they won't cheer Cloud on, I will.' She turned her back on them angrily. 'If it was Minty out in front, they'd cheer loud enough then.'

'Come *on*, Cloud!'

The field reached the second fence, then the third. There was water beyond the third, but the grey landed without making a splash.

'She's made a perfect touchdown,' unconsciously Roma reverted to airline jargon, oblivious of Steve's smile.

'Come *on*, Cloud!'

The crowd began to shout for the grey, and Roma joined in until her voice went hoarse, and her throat felt sore. Four or five horses remained in a tight bunch a length behind, and the rest of the field straggled, out of the running. The filly rose to the fourth fence easily, without apparent effort, and the bunched horses behind followed her over. For a brief second Roma shut her eyes, unable to watch, but when she opened them again the racing horses were safely over, landing together and running on, still keeping station behind the grey.

'Coward!' she derided herself, but she had to make a conscious effort not to shut her eyes again as they reached the final fence. She steeled herself to watch, and felt her palms go wet. Cloud rose first, landed, and raced on unchecked. The first horse of those running behind pecked, spoiling its stride as it landed. The rest of them seemed to explode, and treated Roma to a display of what Steve called 'running off the bit'. It was as if the jockeys suddenly took the brakes off, she thought incredulously. With no more fences to surmount, and a short run in to the winning post, they pulled out all the stops and sprinted for home. To Roma's startled eyes it looked more like a cavalry charge than a race. Her excited shouts died on her lips, and she stared open-mouthed as they careered round the last bend of the track, and one horse emerged from the bunch and left the others standing. Sun glinted on a rich chestnut coat, and caught at the bright silks of the jockey's blouse. Orange vest, and black sleeves. . . .

'It's Mick and Minty! Cloud's first, and Minty's second. . . .'

Even as she cried out, doubt pricked her. It was as if a cold wand of premonition reached out and touched her on the shoulder. There was nothing she could see, no obvious difference in the way the two horses were being ridden, but with turf-devouring strides the chestnut started to overtake the grey. It was as if Mick had been waiting, sitting in behind Cloud and biding his time until the right moment came. It came now.

'Come *on*, Cloud!'

Whether the grey had nothing further to give, or whether the jockey kept her pace controlled, Roma had no means of telling, but with only yards still to go Mick surged out into the lead and put the gelding across the winning line just half a length ahead of Silver Cloud.

It happened so quickly that for a moment or two Roma was unable to take it in. She stared, stunned, at the stragglers still coming in behind, oblivious to the wild shouting of the excited crowd around her. She felt as if she was turned to stone. This, then, was the reason for Earl's silence, the reason for Steve's unemotional dismissal of the grey's performance.

'You knew all along that Cloud wouldn't win.'

The race was ended. It had taken only minutes to run, but she felt as if her life was ended, too. She had accused Earl of cheating, but even when she hurled the accusation at him in the car, she had not really believed in it herself, she did not want to believe it. She had only said it to goad him. Now, her wild words rebounded, mocking her. She felt sick. She did not want to believe, but the evidence was there before her eyes, and would not be denied. There could only be two reasons that would make Earl stoop to malpractice. One was the prize, and he did not need money. The other, she blanched at the thought, the only other reason he could possibly have, was against herself. To prevent her from taking the prize, in order to cut her off from obtaining the means to keep the Lodge. Relentlessly, the reason stared her in the face. She turned tormented eyes on the crowd. No one else appeared to have noticed the trainer's infamy. There was gay chatter and laughter, and called congratulations from those who recognised him, and everyone else seemed happy enough with the result. Certainly Earl looked happy, she saw bitterly. He smiled and nodded, accepting the congratulations. But she, Roma, knew. Anger, and shock, and a desolate feeling of betrayal burned like gall within her. She turned accusing eyes on Earl.

'You knew. . . .' she whispered.

'This way, Guv'nor. You can cut through here to the winners' enclosure.' A gap opened in the fence, revealing a path.

'Come along.' Earl put his hands on her shoulders to guide her through, and she jerked away from his touch, revulsion provoking her into angry speech.

'Take your hands off me!' she hissed at him furiously. 'I won't be a party to your deception. I won't come with you. I don't want to even be *seen* with you!' Tears stung her eyes, and she kept the tremble out of her voice only by a supreme effort. She thrust at his hands, trying to push his fingers away from their grip on her shoulders, but instead of loosening them, they tightened.

'Don't be hysterical.' His eyes were bronze flints, boring into her own. 'There was nothing untoward in the race. You must be mad if you think I'd risk my trainer's licence for the sake of a single race.'

She knew nothing about licences, and cared even less.

'Yes, I am mad,' she flung back at him furiously. Mad with fury, and misery, and disillusion. Fighting mad, and determined to make him pay for what he had done.

'If there was nothing wrong with the race, why didn't Cloud win? Why didn't Bob let her out, the same as the others? She was right out in front of the rest of the field. . . .'

'Cloud was entered to pace the chestnut,' he snapped at her impatiently. 'Steve told you that at dinner last night. I heard him say so myself. You should have listened. . . .' She had heard, but she had not understood. She had not appreciated that there was a difference.

'Steve said Cloud was. . . .'

'Pacing, not racing,' Earl defined the difference for her. 'If it hadn't been for the fact that he had to get away from the loose horse, Bob would have kept to the letter of his instructions and held the animal on the bit. The filly was run to gain experience. Cloud's got to learn her job, she's just an apprentice, the same as the lad who rode her.'

'Then you admit you instructed Bob to lose?' This was monstrous. Her head reeled. He had not even got the grace to try to deny her accusation. He openly admitted. . . .

'I won't stay with you,' she choked, and tried to whirl away. Earl had deceived herself more even than the crowd of racegoers, and relied on her ignorance of the racing world to remain undetected. Through all her dislike of him, she had clung to the belief that at least he was honourable, and now his action made her feel soiled and betrayed.

'You've no choice, unless you intend to buy yourself another passage back across the Channel.' He swung her back to face him. 'I hold the airline tickets, remember?' he gritted.

She had forgotten. Defeated, she stared up at him. Unless she remained with Earl, she would be stranded in France. Unless she remained with Earl, her heart would be stranded anyway, she acknowledged drearily. She thrust the thought aside as Steve called again,

'This way, Guv'nor.' The head lad betrayed impatience as the crowd wandered, filling up the gap.

Earl kept his arm tight about Roma's shoulders, and forced her to walk with him. To the crowd at large, it must have looked as if they were a happy couple, intent on celebrating the trainer's win, she thought bleakly. Her feet dragged, as leaden as her spirits. Bitterly she regretted allowing Steve to add her to the block flight booking, instead of making her own, separate, travel arrangements. If she had held her own ticket she could have left Earl flat, and made public her opinion of his infamous behaviour.

She still could. A thought struck her. She was obliged

to remain with the trainer because of the flight tickets, and his arm around her shoulders, ostensibly to guide her, in reality turned her into a prisoner. But she could still turn his arrogant mastery of the situation to her own advantage, she thought vengefully.

'I won't allow him to get away with it!'

Her steps ceased to drag as she made her plans, and she felt Earl look down at her as she suddenly strode out along with him, no longer resisting the pressure of his arm.

'I'll have to be careful. He mustn't suspect.'

Cautiously she slowed her pace again. The winners' enclosure was just ahead of them, and she scanned it with alert eyes. The set-up seemed to be much the same as on the racecourse in England—the horses walking back from the winning post, Mick, looking for Earl to lead him in. 'The proud owner of the winning horse,' she thought scornfully, and kept her face averted lest her expression betray her. The newspaper reporters were there, waiting with their cameras. This time she welcomed the newspaper reporters. She needed them to carry out her plan.

'I'll denounce him in front of the Press. I'll make him see that he can't manipulate me the same as he manipulated the horses,' she told herself triumphantly. 'It'll be in all the French newspapers, and the English ones too, I shouldn't wonder. I'll make him pay for losing me the race!' She would punish him for trying to wrest her inheritance from her, and for deliberately taking from her the means to keep it.

'We've managed to stay clean this time, Minty and me,' Mick grinned down at them as Earl took the chestnut's head leathers to lead him in. 'Look, no mud,' the jockey quipped.

Mick might be free from mud, but Earl was not, Roma thought darkly. And she intended to see that at least some of it would stick to the trainer's reputation.

'Look this way, Mr Paget. Let us have a picture,' the newspaperman saved her from having to respond. He was English. The familiar tones of the North Country fell upon her ears, and she recognised his face when it emerged from behind his camera as the reporter who had taken their picture before. 'Give us a picture, and a few lines to go with it,' he begged.

This was her opportunity, the moment for her revenge. The presence of the English Press would ensure wide publicity at home, where it would discredit Earl most.

'Give us a caption, Mr Paget,' the reporter urged.

'I'll give you a caption.' Roma spun round to face him, her hands clenched, her whole body rigid with tension. 'When you publish your picture of this man,' she indicated Earl with a scornful toss of her head, 'you can call it, "The face of de. . . ."'

Earl grabbed her before she could complete the sentence. He pulled her into his arms, and swung her to face him, and his lips closed on her own with a kiss that was as savage as a blow. It thrust the word, 'deception' back between her teeth, thrust her revenge back into her throat, while his arms crushed the breath from her lungs with a rib-cracking embrace that held her as if in a vice.

'That's great! Keep it like that for a minute, Mr Paget. Just one more picture. . . .'

Roma tried to struggle free, but she could not move. She tried to cry out, but she could not breathe. Her senses swam, and through a darkening mist she heard the click of the cameras, and then there were no more clicks, only the receding calls of the delighted reporters,

'Thanks, Mr Paget, that was fine!'

'*Merci, monsieur.*'

Another voice, probably from an onlooker, murmured with Gallic sympathy,

'*L'amour.* . . .'

It wasn't love, it was hate. Roma shook with the intensity of her hatred. Desperately she tried to shake her head free, to call out to the departing reporters not to believe the evidence of their own eyes, that this was just another instance of Earl's deception, but his lips clamped limpet-like on top of her own, silencing them with a harsh fury that but for her own passionate anger would have made her afraid.

When he released her, the reporters had gone. Vanished, she saw bitterly, like mist in the wind, in search of telephones to dictate their precious copy, to meet the deadlines of hungry printing machines, to satisfy the needs of an avid public and—she went cold with dismay—to turn her moment of revenge into a boomerang that as soon as the papers were published would rebound on herself far more surely than it would harm Earl.

She reeled against him, half fainting, unable to focus properly, unable to stand. Her legs trembled, and her breath came in shuddering gasps. The racecourse, and the crowd, and the bright sunny afternoon revolved around her, and she shut her eyes and dropped her head against Earl's jacket, berating herself with what little strength she had left for unwittingly adding to the deception by leaning on Earl's arm, as if she wanted to, rather than because if she did not, she would surely fall to the ground.

If only her heart would stop its hopeless pounding! The race was over, but her heart did not know that she had lost. That it had lost. . . . It still raced on, stifling her, choking her, crying out for the touch of his lips, no matter whether they pressed against her own in anger or in love, so long as she could feel his kiss and the pressure of his arms about her. . . .

Someone thrust a glass into her hand. A voice called out cheerfully, 'To Arabian Minty.' Desperate with thirst, she raised the glass to her lips, and gasped as the sharpness of champagne stung her throat. The astringent mouthful cleared her head and put new life into her limbs, and made the world stand still again. She became aware of people talking, speaking to Earl.

'The grey filly's a good mover.' A big, bluff man—she learned later that he was the owner of the loose horse—eyed Earl shrewdly. 'I wouldn't mind making you an offer for her,' he hinted.

It wasn't Earl's place to say whether the grey was for sale or not. It was her horse, not his. Roma tensed, ready to do battle, nerved for it by the heady wine, and then Earl said,

'The filly's not for sale,' and she relaxed again, unwillingly grateful that she did not have to fight on another front. She did not feel she had the strength.

'A pity,' the big man shrugged philosophically. 'How many times have you run her so far?' he asked interestedly.

'Two, up to now.'

It should have been three. It would have been three, if Earl had not scratched her from the last race. Roma opened her mouth to say so, but the stranger spoke before she did.

'Hmmm,' he nodded sagely. 'When she's had one or two more canters like today, to get her used to the feel of things, she'll be ready to make a serious bid for the post.'

For a blank, uncomprehending second, Roma stared at him. His words seemed to bounce about in her mind like so many ping-pong balls, unco-ordinated, directionless, yet pregnant with a meaning she could not grasp, and then he added casually,

'The mount that unshipped its jockey was one of mine. I put it in to pace my second entry, but it didn't do so well as your grey,' he grimaced ruefully.

So he, too, knew that Silver Cloud was not racing to win. Not only that, but he had done exactly the same with one of his own mounts. Realisation dawned upon Roma in a blinding flash. Running a horse as a pacer was accepted practice, not malpractice. The enormity of what she had so nearly done broke over her in a cold wave. If Earl had not stopped her, she would have denounced him in front of the Press of two countries, and all for nothing.

What headlines it would have made! In her mind's eye she could see them, in large black letters on the front pages of all the major national newspapers:

'Trainer denounced for malpractice.'

He would have been exonerated, of course, but like Mick's bright silks, some of the mud would inevitably have stuck, and the stains would show. Perhaps owners would have removed their horses from his stables, maybe per-

manently damaged his business. To a man of Earl's pride,
she knew the damage to his business would matter less
than the stain on his good name. And it would have been
her fault. What folly had her ignorance of the racing world
so nearly led her to commit? In an agony of remorse she
spun round to face him, her hands reaching out, beseech-
ing his forgiveness.

'Earl, I. . . .'

She stammered to a halt as her eyes locked with his. He
made no attempt to catch her hands, and slowly they
dropped to her side, nerveless, rejected.

'So now you know,' he said softly, and his voice was as
hard and as unforgiving as his eyes, which held the
promise—she caught her breath on a sob that was half
remorse and half fear—the promise that he would add
her vengeful intention to the account, and make her pay
the final reckoning in full, deducting nothing at all from
the balance because she had failed in what she set out to
do.

CHAPTER SIX

PARIS!

A city meant for gaiety. A city made for love. Roma's
heart felt as heavy as lead as she walked beside Earl along
the familiar boulevards that she had trodden so often with
a light step in the cheerful company of the airline
crews, happily sightseeing during their brief off-duty
hours.

'There's a couple of hours to kill before the plane leaves.
Let's find somewhere to eat.'

A pavement café beckoned, and Earl steered them towards it, holding out a chair for her, coldly polite, offering
her the courtesy he would accord a stranger. Roma sat
down in silence, dully thankful that Steve and Mick were
with them. The jockey and the head lad kept up a cheerful

flow of talk about the race, unconscious of the war of
feelings that waged like a silent fusillade between herself
and Earl.

'Cloud went well, Roma. She'll make a useful hurdler
by and by.' Unconsciously, Mick rubbed salt into her
wound, emphasising that she could not hope for the filly
to win yet. She had won her first race, but that was only
for novices, like Cloud herself. Success in real racing, if
any, had yet to come.

Mick grinned across the table, unashamedly indulging
himself with a large cream cake now the race was over,
and she managed to smile back, keeping up the brittle
pretence of cheerfulness even though it seemed as if her
face was made of stone, and the effort of forcing a smile
felt as if it would make it crack in two.

'Today's results should give the prices a boost at the
yearling sales tomorrow,' Steve commented in a satisfied
voice. 'We're taking two of our own yearlings in the
morning,' he explained to Roma's enquiring look. 'One
had the same sire as Arabian Minty, so we should have
no trouble in getting a good price for the colt.'

It was shrewd business tactics, Roma acknowledged
flatly. Cause and effect. It presented the sport of kings in
a new, commercial light, one that had not occurred to
her before. But without profit, the sport would founder.
Horses had to be fed, and stable staff paid to look after
them. It all fitted in like a jigsaw puzzle, of which she had
yet only managed to piece together the outline.

'Are you thinking of buying at the sales yourself this
year, Guv'nor?' Mick questioned, and Earl shook his
head.

'Not this time. We've got our hands full with the string
as it is, and two young ones to train up from our own
stud. I'll give it a miss this year.'

Which meant he would not be going to the sales himself.
Roma despised herself for the flood of relief that washed
over her at the news.

'You'd find the sales interesting, Miss Roma.' Was
Steve telepathic, she wondered, that he should offer her

just the escape route she most needed? 'If you come along tomorrow you'll get an insight into what goes on behind the scenes.'

She had already had an insight into what went on behind the scenes, and by her own impulsive action, had nearly caused a calamity as a result, the reckoning for which, she shivered, was still to come.

'I'd love to come along with you,' she rushed into speech, eager not to miss the chance of spending the day away from Burdon Court tomorrow. Of spending the day away from Earl. Anything would serve that took her out of Earl's reach for another day. It was only postponing the inevitable confrontation, but she was willing to grasp at any chance to gain a day's grace. Perhaps in another twenty-four hours she would have a firmer grip of her emotions, and would be able to face Earl with more confidence.

'You three wait for me here.' Roma jumped violently as Earl rose to his feet with unexpected suddenness, as if he had suddenly thought of something, and she had to steel herself to remain still as he added, 'I won't be gone for very long. I'll be back in good time for us to get to the airport.' He did not say where he was going, or why, nor ask them to accompany him, and Roma's resentment flared.

'If he thinks I'm content to kick my heels waiting around until he condescends to come back, he can think again!' she exploded wrathfully, as without even vouchsafing her a nod of farewell, the trainer disappeared among the strolling crowds along the boulevard. 'You can do what you like,' she told Mick and Steve, 'but I'm going to have a walk along and see the shops before we go back.'

'The Guv'nor won't be long,' Mick started dubiously. 'He did say. . . .'

'I don't care what he said.' Nervous tension set Roma's temper on edge. 'He doesn't employ me, and I'm not obliged to carry out his orders,' she stated independently.

'Don't tire yourself, we've got an early start tomorrow,' Steve warned her.

'The earlier the better.' If they started at dawn, it would not be too soon for her. She pushed her chair back into place with an angry thrust.

'Bother!'

Her impatient movement brought her wrist watch into contact with the metal table top with a sharp bang.

'Has it broken the glass?' The jockey voiced her own concern.

'No.' She ran her finger over the watch face, and breathed a sigh of relief. 'It's still intact, thank goodness.' She waved an airy hand at the two. 'Don't put on too much weight,' she warned Mick flippantly, and set off along the boulevard with her head held high. The street was lined with shops, and she turned to inspect a dress draped in elegant solitude across the window of the first one. It was made from the finest silk, bore the name of a famous fashion house, and was every woman's dream of a gown. So why was it that Earl's face superimposed itself between her eyes and the dress? Why did his voice speak in her ears, instead of the cheerful noise from the crowd promenading along the boulevard?

'So now you know....'

She gave herself a mental shake and walked on restlessly, forcing herself to stop in front of each dress shop window, and examine the display with minute attention, even though what she saw failed to register in her mind, and she could not afterwards remember what it was she had looked at with such close attention, or how long she had remained staring unseeing at the work of the world's top dress designers. It seemed like a very long time. She looked at her watch to confirm how long, and her mind registered dull surprise.

'I haven't been many minutes. I've got plenty of time to walk to the end of the row of shops before I go back.' She did not want to go back too soon, otherwise she would get there before Earl, and he would not know she had gone, and her stand for independence would have been wasted. Deliberately she forced herself to remain for several minutes looking in each shop as she came to it, until she came to the end of the row, where she turned.

'I'll go back now.' She had given the trainer sufficient time to return to the café and find her missing, enough to prove her point. She checked with her watch again, to make sure she had used up enough time, glanced at it, paused, and looked again, harder this time, staring at it with numb disbelief.

'It's stopped!'

Her eyes widened with dismay. The tiny fingers still stood at the position they had occupied when she had checked the time before. That must have been . . . how long ago?

'It must have stopped when I banged it against the table,' she muttered worriedly, and stood undecided, biting her lip. It was a considerable distance back to the café, and depending on how long she had taken to wander among the shops, there might not be time to go back. If she did go back, probably Mick and Steve would not be there. They would assume, because she had not returned, that she had decided to go on to the airport alone, to assert her independence of Earl. She had not bothered to hide her anger at being told to wait for him.

'I wish I knew what time it was.' Earl said there were two hours to go before the plane left, and they had sat drinking coffee for nearly half an hour before she set off on her shopgazing expedition. Thoroughly worried now, she glanced round her, but none of the buildings boasted a public clock. A woman approached from the opposite direction, holding a child by the hand, and Roma waylaid her.

'*Quelle heure est-il?*'

The woman smiled, told her the time, and walked on, and Roma just had the presence of mind to stammer,

'*Merci. . . .*' before her mind went blank with pure panic. She had been shopgazing for nearly an hour. No wonder it had seemed a long time! How could she have been so foolish? she berated herself wretchedly. Not only

had she laid herself open to justifiable criticism on the
trainer's part, by defying him she could very well have
left herself stranded in Paris. Earl held the tickets, and
there were only twenty-five short minutes before the plane
left. It had taken them a good quarter of an hour, she
remembered, to get from the airport to the racecourse, on
the outward journey.

'Taxi!'

She signalled a passing cab with a frantically waving
hand. If he failed to stop, she would be too late. He
stopped. With a squeal of brakes he lurched to a halt, and
Roma gabbled breathless directions. With a gasp of relief
she subsided into the seat, and had to grab for the side as
the driver started off at hair-raising speed.

'I should have known better than to tell a French taxi
driver to get a move on!' she groaned. He took her instructions literally, and with regrettable enthusiasm.
Acting on the assumption that the needs of his fare put
him above the law, he screeched round the corner with a
noise that made Roma wince for his tyres; avoided a bus
with a swerve that detached her from her hold and sent
her sliding to the other end of the seat, and rounded a
policeman on point duty at a speed that Roma felt sure
would cost him his licence if the arm of the law had time
to notice his number.

'I want to get to the airport alive, as well as on time,'
she protested in desperation, and immediately regretted
speaking. At the sound of her voice the driver turned his
head, and looked back at her. 'Mind this other taxi in
front! Look out!' Frantically she directed his attention
back to where it belonged, but she was seconds too late.
Both the taxis swerved, both vehicles touched. It was only
a slight, glancing blow. It did not upset the equilibrium
of either vehicle, and merely added another very slight
dent each to the respective bumpers, which already bore
multitudinous scars of similar encounters much worse than
this one.

The inevitable happened. At any other time Roma
would have regarded the ensuing hassle as just an every-

day part of the Paris scenery. But not now. Both the drivers jumped out of their cabs, and began to shout and
gesticulate. Roma jumped out too, and tried to re-
monstrate with them, but she stood no chance. They were
enjoying themselves far too much. The argument had not
even begun to warm up yet. It was like watching a ritual
dance, she thought desperately, and knew from past experience that it would continue for at least another ten
minutes, long enough to destroy any hope she might have
of getting to the airport on time.

'I told you to wait for me at the café.'

Earl thrust an impatient fist into his pocket and brought
it out with sufficient francs clutched in his fingers to silence
even the two taxi drivers. With deliberate policy he thrust
it into the hands of her own taxi driver, thus accomplish-
ing two things at once. It released her from any obligation
to settle her fare, and cut off the two drivers' time-con-
suming demands that she be a witness as to which was the
one responsible for the collision. They immediately forgot
their argument on that particular score, and started another as to who should have the lion's share of the francs.
At any other time Earl's tactics would have amused
Roma, but he gave her no time to see the humour of the
situation. With a curt order to 'Get in,' and without
waiting to see if she was willing to comply, he bundled
her into his own taxi, whose meter was still busily ticking
away nearby. It was practically abduction. Roma thought
indignantly. She had not even noticed him arrive on the
scene until he was actually beside her, and taking charge.
She tried not to be thankful that he had come, and that
he did take charge. The taxi shot away from the kerb and
pushed her back into the seat with a breath-expelling
thrust as he said,

'I told you to wait for me at the café!' He turned on
her before the door had scarcely shut behind him.

'And I chose not to,' Roma flashed back through set
teeth. 'I'm not a child, to be told to sit and wait until I'm
collected.'

'Then don't behave like one,' he thrust back at her

cuttingly. 'So far today,' he cut short her angry protest as if she had not spoken, and swept on accusingly, 'so far today you've accused me of rigging a race, you've done your best to publicly wreck my career as a trainer, and all because of some crazy misconception you've got into your head about a sport about which you know absolutely nothing, and now, to cap it all, you've nearly succeeded in making us miss the plane back home. For one day, that isn't bad going,' he finished scathingly.

If it had not been for Earl's timely intervention, Roma would have succeeded in making them miss the plane back home. She did not know whether to feel relieved or sorry that he had turned up and rescued her in the nick of time.

'It's your own fault,' she refused to accept the blame, even for trying to denounce him. He should have explained to her what it was all about, and he had not bothered. He had not thought her worth an explanation.

'My fault?' His brows drew together in a scowl that resembled a winter sky, but by now Roma was beyond caring or caution. She felt emotionally worn out by the upheavals of the day, alternatively exhilarated and frightened, uplifted and chastened, her sorely tried temper reached breaking point, and snapped.

'You should have explained to me what you were going to do. You must have known the impression it would give, to someone who knew nothing about racing.' Ignorance was not a crime, she told herself passionately. Earl would be in just such a quandary on airline practice. 'I *am* Silver Cloud's owner,' she reminded him imperiously, 'but you couldn't be bothered to explain. You didn't think it was worth while. . . .' She could not bring herself to voice what she really meant: 'You didn't think *me* worth while. . . .'

Her throat constricted, unable to say the words, and she started to turn her head away lest he should detect the quiver in her voice, and the sharp salt sting of tears that made her eyes over-bright, and blurred the world outside the cab window so that she was unprepared when the driver swung his wheel, and without slackening speed put the cab into a right-angled turn that was as reckless as the progress of her previous transport.

'Madman!' Earl shouted, and caught her as she slid across the seat. She landed heavily against him. She could not help herself. Something hard in his pocket, that felt like the corner of a box, dug into her ribs, and his arms closed round her, holding her tightly against him as the cab lurched upright again and careered on its way. A familiar way. Roma recognised the approach to the airport. In another couple of hundred yards they would be inside the entrance gates, nearly at the terminal building. And she was practically lying across Earl's lap.

'Loose me,' she hissed at him urgently. 'Help me up!'

'Why should I?' Infuriatingly, he seemed to be in no great hurry to comply. The corner of the box, or whatever it was his pocket held, dug uncomfortably against her ribs, goading her to move, but Earl's arm was heavy across her, and in the swaying cab she could find no hand hold except Earl himself to push herself upright again.

'For goodness' sake, let me go!' Her face went scarlet, and her patience gave way. 'Haven't you done enough damage already, by giving the newspaper reporters that— that—picture, on the racecourse?' she burst out bitterly. He had criticised her behaviour, but his own was even worse.

'If you're worried about the damage the newspaper photograph might do to your reputation,' his eyes glinted with a steely light, 'may I remind you that you tried to do a good deal more damage, to mine?'

She did not want to think about it, let alone to be reminded of it. In desperation she tried another tack.

'What will Mick and Steve think if they see us like this?' she pleaded urgently. 'We're nearly at the terminal buildings. They might be waiting for us outside.'

'I've no idea what Mick and Steve might think,' Earl observed interestedly, 'but let's give them something to start on, shall we?' and he lowered his head.

Kissing in the back of a taxi in broad daylight might be excusable for a honeymoon couple, Roma thought in

panic, but for a pair of returning racegoers with only
minutes to spare in which to catch their plane home, it
was . . . it was. . . .

'Bliss!' sighed her heart, contentedly.

She was cradled in his arms, half lying across his lap
where she had fallen, and her upturned face was a perfect
target for his seeking lips. They wandered slowly, exploring her eyes, her temples, savouring the sweet, flooding
tide of colour that blushed her throat and cheeks to a
delicate, shy rose.

'Don't,' she murmured, 'people will see.' But her protest
lacked conviction, and her lips themselves contradicted
the words even as they uttered them. They turned eagerly,
responding to the demand of his, to the heady, passionate
enchantment of his kiss, that made sudden magic between
them, binding her in its spell as his mouth sought and
clung to her own, hungry, demanding. It bewitched her
into forgetting such mundane things as interested on-
lookers, and times of planes back home, and the corner of
a box that dug bruises into her ribs. It filled her horizon,
her whole world, with only one thing,

'Earl,' she whispered huskily, and her arms rose to clasp
him even more closely to her.

'That should give Mick and Steve something to occupy
their minds on the journey back home,' he said, and sat
her upright with a swift lift, off his lap and back on to the
seat beside him, in a single, decisive movement that tore
away her clinging arms, and left her lips in mid-seeking,
wide open, like her eyes, with the pain of brutal separation.

'We've got exactly five minutes to catch the plane,' he
stated practically, and added over his shoulder to her as
he leaned forward to speak to the driver, 'Carry on along
with Steve and Mick. Don't wait for me, I'll catch up
with you.'

Mick stepped forward as the taxi drew to a halt at the
paved front of the terminal building, and wrenched open
the door of the cab even as Earl dug his hand into his
pocket to pay their fare. Roma sat where he had put her,

speechless, frozen, her eyes enormous in her face, from which all vestige of colour had fled.

'Earl, you . . . I. . . .'

'Get a move on, or we'll miss the plane,' he interrupted her brusquely. 'I told you, I'll catch up with you. Now go on, *run*!'

She ran.

Mick held her by the one hand, and Steve held her by the other, and she ran between the jockey and the head lad, clinging on to them, not daring to let go, because her numbed mind could not remember the well-known route, and her blinded eyes could not see to direct her for the tears that washed her cheeks like rain.

She ran with Mick and Steve. Away from Earl. Away from the moment of enchantment that lay shattered behind her, smashed like a bright, shiny bauble from a Christmas tree. Broken, in as many pieces as her heart.

CHAPTER SEVEN

'MR HORACE BLANTYRE's on the telephone again, Mr Paget.' Mrs Murray sounded resigned.

'Owners! There ought to be a law against them!' Earl pushed aside his plate with an angry thrust. 'That's four times Blantyre's called me within twenty-four hours,' he exploded irately, and jumped to his feet, leaving his bacon and eggs to congeal on their plate as he quitted the breakfast table with only the briefest of apologies to Roma and Steve.

It was very late by the time they returned the night before, and in view of their early start for the yearling sales, the head lad had remained overnight at Burdon Court, a reprieve for which Roma felt everlastingly grateful. To sit beside Earl on the plane returning from Paris had been an almost unendurable strain. For most of the time she kept her eyes closed, pretending to sleep, anything rather than try to keep up a stilted conversation that dared not voice the words that lay between them, the feelings that lay in her heart. To have returned to the house on her own with Earl afterwards would have been more than she could bear.

The moment they got inside, she pleaded tiredness and went straight upstairs to her room, leaving Earl talking with Steve, and the head lad was already at the breakfast table when she got down that morning. For the first time since she had been at Burdon Court, Earl was late for breakfast. She knew he had not left his room, she heard him moving about farther along the corridor as she shut her own door and came downstairs. She neither knew nor cared what reason had caused him to forsake his habitual punctuality, so long as that reason kept her from being alone with him.

'The Guv'nor sounds put out,' Steve remarked unnecessarily, as a loud clatter wafted through the doorway from the hall where Earl picked up the receiver from the telephone table. His voice came back sharply to them.

'Paget here.' He spoke shortly, with barely concealed impatience, and went on after a short pause, 'Yes, I know. But Night Sky is perfectly fit now. His indisposition was only temporary. It was colic, caused by his greedy feeding habits.' The speaker did not try to hide his disgust, Roma thought with an inner quirk of amusement. It was some satisfaction to know that not everything went according to Earl's plans, either. 'I'm aware of that.' Again the barely concealed impatience.

'His bacon and egg's getting cold,' Roma noticed with an inward grin, and pricked her ears interestedly as the trainer went on,

'If a horse bolts its food, it gets wind, the same as a human being would, and suffers in consequence. The animal was given a drench, and it's proved effective. I checked the colt personally at the stables this morning, and it's well and comfortable, and resting quietly in its stall. It will go out to exercise with the rest of the string in the normal way, later this morning.'

'Night Sky?' Roma mouthed a silent question at Steve.

'The big black colt with the white sock.' Steve's lips quirked in an answering grin. 'The owner's a business man with plenty of money, and the horse is his hobby,' he elucidated. 'It's also the apple of his eye. And a speck of grit in the Guv'nor's,' he added with a chuckle.

'Isn't the horse any good?' Roma remembered the colt well enough. She had reason to, she thought ruefully. It was the one which nearly trampled her in the stable yard.

'The colt's fine, it's got good potential as a hurdler, and it's already won three races, and got placed in two more. But the owner's an absolute blight.' The head lad's sympathy was patently with the trainer. 'He rings up the Guv'nor at all hours of the day and night to make sure his precious racehorse is still ticking over as it should. He's as fussy as a mother hen with one chick.' He stopped speaking as Earl reappeared through the breakfast room door, and flung himself back into his chair in an excess of exasperation.

'The times I've told that man,' he growled irritably, and pushed away his ruined breakfast with a grimace. 'If there's one thing worse than having an owner totally uninterested in anything connected with his horse, except for the prize money it wins, it's having one breathing down your neck and pestering you night and day with silly questions.'

'Or even worse, living in the same house with you?' Roma murmured sweetly. She did not feel sweet. She felt like a kettle boiling furiously with the lid about to pop off. The trainer was insufferably rude, she thought angrily. She was a racehorse owner as well, so what he said must apply to herself as much as it did to the unknown Horace Blantyre. 'Racehorse owners provide you with your living,' she reminded him tartly. She did not believe what she said to be strictly true. From what the solicitor had implied, Earl's private means were more than adequate to provide him with his bread and butter. Training racehorses merely added a liberal supply of jam, and, she suspected, provided him with an occupation that was as much a hobby to him as a job.

'Airline passengers *used* to provide you with your living,' he put biting emphasis on the 'used' and Roma flushed angrily, 'but you wouldn't have been human if you didn't prefer some to others,' he retorted.

'Perhaps Mr Blantyre will feel a bit happier if the black wins his next race,' Steve put in placatingly. 'It's disappointing for the owner if the horse doesn't win,' he said sympathetically, and turned to Roma with a smile. 'We'll find something for you today to make up for Cloud not winning yesterday,' he promised kindly. 'Now I must be off, I want to see the two yearlings safely boxed. I'm using the split box, it'll pull easily behind the Range Rover,' he suggested to Earl.

'That's fine by me,' Earl nodded his permission, and the head lad pushed his chair back, preparing to depart on his errand.

'I'll go upstairs and get ready.' Roma abandoned her coffee, and made good her escape before Steve had time to leave the room. With luck Earl would finish his coffee and go back to the stables again before she came downstairs. She hummed to herself as she pulled on her black slacks and white silk top, and fished the pale blue sweater from out of her dressing table drawer. It would not matter if she did look only sixteen years old today, when she was with Steve, she told herself happily. She did not need to wear armour when she was with the head lad. She only needed to erect defences around herself when she was with Earl. She tugged the sweater over her head, straightened the collar of her blouse over the top, and turned to the dressing table to reach for her comb.

'What . . .?'

Her hand arrested in mid-air, and she stared at the small blue and gold box that sat in the middle of her vanity tray. It had not been there when she came downstairs to breakfast.

'That isn't the box to Flip's perfume.' His box had been an explosion of vivid orange and black. Rather like the perfume itself, she smiled wryly, and reached for the delicately patterned blue and gold box with curious fingers.

'Fleur. . . .' She recognised the name of the world-famous Paris perfumer that sold only, 'Cosmetics, made from floral essences. Of course!' she exclaimed softly, and her face lit up with a pleased smile.

'Steve and Mick remembered.' Steve had said they would find something to make up to her for Cloud not winning at Auteuil yesterday. This must be their answer.

'Bless them for being kind!' The small warm glow of their kindness eased away some of the bleakness that had taken possession of her heart, and she unscrewed the tiny cap and pressed the atomiser, gently this time, careful not to spray the contents too liberally on her wrist, remembering the hasty overdose on that other, disastrous occasion.

'Mmmm, this is lovely!'

Flip's perfume had been cloying, exotic, suited to the sophisticated life style enjoyed by the donor. This was light, and fresh, and clean-smelling, an out-of-doors scent, redolent of the bright sweet warmth of summer meadows, and cool, perfume-haunted cottage gardens after dusk. Somehow Mick and Steve had guessed just the sort of perfume she liked, and their thoughtful action put a lift into her step as she thrust her arms into her anorak, and ran downstairs. Earl was gone. She did not wait to find out where, but hurried to discover Steve already waiting by the Range Rover.

'I didn't think you'd be ready yet.' She cast a surprised look at the horsebox hitched on to the back of the vehicle. 'Are the yearlings . . .?'

'Safely boxed,' Steve confirmed with a grin. 'A carrot's a wonderful inducement.'

'I shan't need one to get in here.' Roma swung happily up into the passenger seat of the Range Rover, and hitched the seat belt round her. A day away from Earl's company was inducement enough, she thought grimly, and snuggled back comfortably into the luxurious upholstery as Steve made his way round to the driver's side.

'We'll be away in good time.' The head lad opened the driver's door and turned a cheerful face up to Roma. 'That smell's nice,' he sniffed appreciatively.

'It's my new perfume.' Roma smiled back at him. 'It's a lovely scent, Steve, just what I like. It's a lovely gift,' she began gratefully.

'I reckon the Guv'nor won two races in one day yesterday, to get to Fleur's in time to collect the perfume he'd ordered,' Steve laughed. 'It must be at least six blocks away from where we sat at that café table, and to get there and back in under thirty minutes, during the evening rush hour, is some achievement,' he said admiringly.

'Earl ordered it?' Roma gazed at him blankly.

'Yes, he gave them a ring before we started out yesterday morning,' Steve grinned, enjoying the secret, enjoying its success. 'I'm glad you like it. So will the Gov'nor be,' he said happily.

She had almost thanked Steve for the perfume. The words of gratitude still trembled on the tip of her tongue. She felt herself go pink with embarrassment. What would the head lad have thought, if the words had been spoken? He would probably have been as embarrassed as she was herself. Earl should not have put her in such a position, she levelled the blame at the trainer, angrily thrusting away the memory of his unusually late arrival at the breakfast table, and then finding the perfume on her dressing table when she returned to her room afterwards. Hindsight told her she should have guessed who the donor was.

'It was the possibility of you coming with us today to the sales, I expect,' Steve said with naïve frankness. 'It reminded him.'

Roma did not need to be reminded. The memory of what happened in the stable yard made her go pinker still. She had not worn Flip's perfume since. She did not intend to, ever again. But also she did not intend to allow Earl to dictate to her what perfume she *should* use. His gift was tantamount to ordering her what to put on, she told herself furiously. Or perhaps a sop to his conscience, be-

cause his horse had won the race yesterday, instead of her
own? That must have been the small, hard box in his
pocket, that dug into her ribs in the taxi. She closed her
mind to the memory of it, the pain. . . .

'I'll give it back to him the very minute we get back
this evening,' she vowed. 'The very *second*. . . .'

'It's time I joined you.' Steve tilted the back of the
driver's seat, and slid the unit forward in its runners, then
ducked through the wide aperture and swung himself up
into the back seat, pulling the driving seat back into position. 'Here comes the Guv'nor,' he said.

'I thought he was staying at home?' Her dismayed ears
caught the sound of Earl's step on the cobbles of the stable
yard. 'You said . . . I thought. . . .' A cold sense of finality
gripped her as Steve said,

'The Guv'nor's driving,' and added thankfully, 'He's
welcome, so far as I'm concerned. I can drive anything
with four legs, but four wheels defeats me,' he confessed.
'Six wheels, if you count the trailer on the back.'

If she had known, she would not have come. She could
so easily have remained at Burdon Court for the day,
perhaps walked along to look at the Lodge. Earl's step
beside the open door told her it was too late now to change
her mind. His face appeared in the opening, and his voice
asked briskly,

'All set?'

Roma wished she had not come. She wished she had
not worn Earl's perfume. He must be able to smell it, the
light sweetness of it hung delicately on the air inside the
vehicle. He could not miss it. He had not missed it. He
turned to look at her as he swung himself up behind the
steering wheel, a long, enigmatic look that told her he
recognised the scent, and knew she liked it, and took it for
granted that she would wear it, and no other. She longed
to get out her handkerchief and rub at her wrists to
remove it, to demonstrate her independence, and knew
with growing chagrin that it was too late to do that, as
well.

'They're getting on with the Lodge—look, they've got

the thatch off the roof already.' Steve diverted her
thoughts as Earl cautiously slowed their mini convoy at
the near approach to the drive gates, and involuntarily
Roma turned her head to see. She did not want to show
interest in front of Earl, in case it might heighten the
impression that she was anxious, for financial reasons, to
have the Lodge completed, but Steve's ejaculation took
her unawares, and she looked before she coould stop herself. 'They've got some good reed for the new roof,' the
head lad went on with critical approval. 'It looks as if
they intend to start thatching today.'

The sight of the new, pale covering for the Lodge should
have given her pleasure. She recognised the pressures,
both on economic and quality grounds, that demanded
her inheritance be clothed in reed and not in straw, but
the fact that it was reed still rankled. The material of the
thatcher's art lay stacked beside the Lodge, silently ac-
claiming Earl's victory, and her lips tightened as the
Range Rover rolled slowly to the T-end that joined the
drive with the lane.

'Keep an eye open to the left for me,' Earl cut across
her thoughts. Roma did not know whether he spoke to
herself or to the head lad, it could have been either, but
she bristled resentfully at his curt order, her feelings rasped
still further by her own inability to stop her instinctive
glance to check the lane on their left. 'This turn out on to
the lane will have to be altered,' Earl went on. 'The height
of the Lodge hedge means you're driving blind, straight
on to a bend.'

'That's what I'm doing,' Roma thought disconsolately.
The overhanging trees cut off the early sun, and cast long
fingers of shadow across the small, stone built house she
would soon be able to call home. The shadow seemed to
her heightened imagination to be like some dark omni-
presence, brooding over the skeleton roof, its timbers
sticking out like gaunt bones where the thatch had been
stripped away ready to take the new covering.

'I'm driving blind, into the future.' It was a frightening
thought, and she shivered. She had come to a bend in her

own personal road, and difficulties and decisions hedged her in, blocking off the view, so that she did not know in which direction to turn. Earl did not share her uncertainty. He told her bluntly.

'Go back to your airliners, and the world you know.'

But the world she knew did not beckon to her any longer, and to go back to it would mean leaving Earl behind.

'The road's clear to your left,' Steve intoned, and Earl swung the wheel, and they were on their way to Newmarket, and the yearling sales, and it was Earl instead of Steve who was at the wheel. She hoped fervently that the head lad would remain with them during the course of the sales.

'Have you brought enough money with you, in case you have to stay overnight?' Earl spoke over his shoulder to Steve.

'Plenty, though I may not have to,' Steve answered. 'I phoned the suppliers this morning, and they said they'd have the sample harnesses waiting for me when I got there, and with a bit of luck I'll be able to leave our order with them and catch the evening train back. There's a straight through train to Down Burdon at eight-fifteen.'

'Aren't you coming to the sales?' Roma swallowed hard. She felt like she had done once when she was at school, and she had been taken out for a treat, only to discover that the grown-ups had carefully omitted to mention a visit to the dentist en route. Steve's continued presence was her only insulator against the electric tension that continually sparked between herself and Earl, and erupted in sudden, lightning flashes whenever they were alone together, precursors of the looming storm that gathered around them, and built up inside herself. The Lodge merely acted as a smouldering fuse attached to the dynamite of emotional tension that threatened to explode her life into a thousand fragments, and which helplessly she knew herself unable to extinguish, because the fire that fed it burned fiercely within herself, consuming her thoughts, her will, yet seeming unable to ignite even an answering flicker in Earl.

On the return journey from Newmarket that evening, Steve would not be with them. He would be on his way to the train if his business for the stables was completed, and she would be faced with the journey back to Burdon Court, alone with Earl, and she would have no defence against the trainer's hostility, and even worse, she thought despairingly, no defence against herself.

'I'll stay until after our own horses are dealt with, then I want to get off to the suppliers as quickly as I can,' Steve answered her nonchalantly, and could not know what a leaden weight his words left in her stomach. 'The journey doesn't seem to have bothered them at all.' The head lad let down the back of the horsebox to form a ramp, and backed out a young, dun-coloured horse, while Earl took charge of the other one, that was, she thought with a sudden catch in her throat, a younger replica of Arabian Minty.

'It seems dreadful to rear them, and then have to let them go. Not to know what happens to them afterwards.' She felt herself assailed by an unaccountably choky sensation as she watched the two untried youngsters, who by the time the day was over would have different owners, and new homes to get used to.

'It doesn't pay to get emotionally involved with the animals,' Earl retorted crisply, and added, 'Don't stand in front of them. Never stand in front of a yearling.'

'Does everything have to pay?' she flashed back, but she moved out of the way nevertheless, resenting his order, yet respecting it, cautious since her experience in the stable yard, noting Steve's quiet rider, 'They're liable to rear, miss. To all intents and purposes they're still wild, you see, are yearlings. They haven't been broken yet.'

Why couldn't Earl have gone to the trouble to explain? she asked herself vexedly. Steve bothered to, so why didn't Earl?

'Everything has to pay in a business,' the trainer retorted, 'or the stud would soon go bankrupt. And we don't exactly lose sight of them,' he added drily. 'These aren't ordinary hacks, they're registered thoroughbreds, and at the prices they'll fetch today their new owners won't be inclined to neglect them. They'll be well looked after, don't worry, if only to protect the owner's investment. . . . Whoa!' He broke off as the young chestnut skittered, nervous of the unaccustomed bustle of its surroundings after the peace of its home pastures, soothing it with quiet words, his whole attention on the animal, forgetting Roma. A stab of pain pierced her as she watched him, a yearning that became an anguish because the strange, elusive gentleness that lay beneath the strong, hard exterior of this man, seemed to surface so readily when he was with the horses, but never when he was with herself.

The animals had been superlatively well looked after up until now, Roma acknowledged. Even her untutored eyes could see that they were both in prime condition, and the horsebox was the last word in equine luxury. No expense had been spared to make the journey free from stress for the occupants. A middle partition divided the box into two cubicles, the walls of which were rugged to make them soft if the animals should lean against them. There was ample room for comfort, but not so much that the four-footed passengers would be tossed about if the trailer encountered sharp bends along the road. The trailer was fine, but—emotional involvement?

Was Earl capable of emotional involvement? Roma asked herself drearily. With people, as well as with animals? And felt the bright autumn sunshine grow dim as, search as she might, the only answer she could find was, 'no'.

'I'll get the yearlings settled, then I can come back and watch the bidding with you for a little while,' said Steve, and Roma heaved a sigh of relief that she would not be left alone with Earl for a little while, at least.

'Ours go up in Lot No. Seven,' Steve consulted his catalogue a short while later. 'Here they are, on this line,' he steered Roma through the technicalities. 'The write-up here gives the animal's pedigree, and the history of the sire and the dam. If you want to pick a future winner,' he

advised her teasingly, 'go for an animal with a winner on
the dam's side.'

'That should make it easy,' Roma entered into the spirit
of the thing and scanned his list eagerly. 'That one looks
as if it should be good, and that one. . . .'

'There's a lot more to it than that.' Earl bent a look on
her that held lurking amusement, and something else that
she was unable to define, something that made her
suddenly unable to meet his eyes, so that she had to turn
her own in confusion back to the catalogue. 'You need to
look at the animal itself, at its conformation. . . .'

His conformation was perfect. Roma eyed him covertly.
He was tall, and straight, and he carried not a surplus
ounce on his lean frame, his fine bones and proudly
carried head proclaiming him to be as much a thoroughbred as the horses he trained.

'The first one is from an Irish stud,' Steve guided her
attention to the commencement of activities in the ring,
forcing her to concentrate on the leggy brown yearling
that was being paced by its lad for the benefit of the
surrounding bidders. The voice of the auctioneer droned
into the sudden intent silence, and the bids rose sharply;
Roma noticed they still went in the old-fashioned guineas,
not in pounds, and they rose to a hitherto undreamed-of
level.

'I never knew a horse could cost so much,' she breathed
at last, awestruck, as the first horse was taken out, having
found an owner, and another animal brought in and the
whole process began over again.

'It's a calculated risk,' Earl told her, his eyes keen on
the ring. 'If a horse subsequently does well, your investment pays off. If not. . . .' He shrugged philosophically.

This, then, was the hard core of racing she was being
initiated into. The under-the-surface risk business that the
general public did not usually see. It was a quicksand
that could swallow a man into bankruptcy unless he had
a shrewd eye and an unerring judgment for the horses
which were his stock in trade. It was a world that was not
for an amateur. In spite of her determination not to show

any interest, the fascination of it drew Roma, absorbed her, so that she felt herself carried away by the tensely charged atmosphere, as knowledgeable men bid against one another, and on their hopes for the future.

'What points do you look for?' The question came out of its own accord, her mind keen to learn. The racecourse itself, she realised now, was merely the end product, the tip of the iceberg, and the only part that reached the eye of the racing public, although in fact it was merely a surface icing on a very solid cake of underlying skill, sound judgment, and sheer dedicated hard work.

'It's a fairly sound rule of thumb when you're buying a horse, to avoid the points you'd distrust in a man.' The amusement was evident in Earl's eyes now, he did not try to hide it. He looked down at Roma, and laughter glinted like sun-specks in their clear brown. Laughter at her ignorance of his world? Mocking her, for what to him must seem a naïve question? Taunting her for not belonging to his world, from the certain knowledge that she would never belong there, because he himself was her only door to that world, and he kept it tightly shut, and herself on the outside, hopelessly knocking and receiving no answer. She stared back at him in silent resentment, hating him for laughing at her, for debarring her from his world—from himself. Her hatred rose like gall inside her. She longed to shout at him that he could keep his world, that she did not want to share in it, or in him, that she would go back to her own world, to the one she knew.

But the words would not come, because she knew she could not go back, would not, because by going back she would cut herself off from Earl, and that she could not bear. But by staying, she would condemn herself to living in a desolate no man's land between the two worlds, empty, bereft, denied both consolation and the bright fulfilment of her secret dreams, wandering like a wraith into an empty future until at last the dreams faded, withered like a dried seed husk, capable of feeling neither love nor pain. Numbly she heard Earl continue his tutorage, but the words seemed to bounce back off her mind, uncomprehended, because they were not the words she longed to hear.

'Avoid the horse with small pig eyes,' he said, 'or a receding forehead. And never mount a horse with a bump between its eyes, you'll find yourself on top of a rogue.'

Easy words. Nonsense words. Surely he did not expeect her to believe such nonsense? Tears pricked her eyes at his mockery, and she turned her head away.

'He's got a fine instinct for a promising horse, has Mr Paget.' A man at the ringside turned and spoke, nodding recognition to Earl, appraising herself, confirming that what Earl told her was not nonsense, but established fact, and words to be listened to and heeded if she wanted to learn. The stranger was breeched and tweeded, and had a nut-brown, wrinkled face, and he had just bought the yearling that was even now being led from the ring. He was an obvious part of this alien world which Roma so longed to enter and could not. 'I've never known Earl to buy a bad one yet,' he said sagely, and Roma sensed he was not using flattery, but merely speaking the truth. He did not look as if he even knew what flattery was. Roma liked him on sight, and somehow managed a smile, which encouraged him to add wistfully, 'Add a load of luck to a promising yearling, and you get that rare thing, a super racehorse.'

'Super racehorse owners are even more rare.'

She turned and stared at Earl, her eyes wide with the shock of his words. He spoke so softly that they barely reached her, could not possibly have reached anyone else, so they must be meant for her ears alone. He did not bother to qualify them by adding, 'present company excepted, of course,' he just let the words hang in the air between them, rawly challenging.

Roma drew in a quivering breath, and her face went slowly white, drained of all its colour except for a small, bright spot of red on either cheek, like the marks left by a cruel hand after a physical blow. Anger erupted in her. It gathered to itself all the resentment and the misery and the pain, and spilled over like the rumblings of a mighty storm. It turned her eyes black with passion until they glowed like living coals in her bloodless face. He never missed a chance to strike, she thought furiously. Even on a day out, among a crowd of people, Earl took his opportunity to hurt. But she could strike back. Her voice shook as she retaliated.

'Super racehorse trainers are non-existent!' she hissed back at him furiously. The moment she had legal control of Silver Cloud, she would remove her horse from his stables, she promised herself wrathfully. She would not leave Silver Cloud at Burdon Court a moment longer than she was obliged to by the terms of her godfather's will. She would not subject herself to this cat-and-mouse game of torture a moment longer than she had to.

'I'm off,' Steve butted in without warning, and added with a grimace, 'Here comes Mr Blantyre, Guv'nor. The owner of the black colt,' he explained for Roma's benefit. 'The one who keeps ringing up about his horse. He's all yours, Guv'nor,' he abdicated any claim to remain and speak with the owner.

'I know, I spotted him coming through the crowd towards us, a couple of minutes ago,' Earl said resignedly.

'I'm going, before he spots me,' the head lad said with frank distaste. 'I've got to go anyway, because of our two yearlings,' he presented a watertight excuse for his defection.

'Mind you show off their paces properly,' Earl began automatically, but the head lad had vanished into the crowd, and Roma turned in time to confront a portly, pink and white individual whose puffily fat cheeks and hands, and air of aggressive opulence, made her dislike him on sight.

'Ah, Paget!' The stout owner waved his newspaper at Earl. 'I thought I might catch you here today.'

Roma stole a glance at Earl's face, and smothered a grin. 'Catch' was the operative word, she thought maliciously. The trainer's face reflected the same expression as that of his head lad.

'I wanted to know about Night Sky. . . .'

Since the owner had only that morning been told, Roma felt a sneaking sympathy with the barely restrained exasperation in Earl's voice as he replied,

'The colt's in perfect health. I explained that to you this morning. In fact, Night Sky is due to race in two days' time at Cheltenham. You were informed,' he said coldly.

'I'll be there,' Horace Blantyre promised, and added with a wink, 'I thought you might be good for a few tips off the cuff, so to speak.'

'Look, Steve's in the ring with one of our colts.' Roma could see no good reason why she should help Earl out of his difficulty, but she did. She grasped the trainer's arm, and cut across the other owner's conversation with a lack of manners that at any other time would have made her feel ashamed. Now she put it down to a worthy cause, and felt unrepentant.

'Lot No. Seven, sent up by the Burdon Court Stud,' intoned the auctioneer, and started the bidding at five hundred guineas. Roma gasped. Six hundred ... seven hundred ... eight hundred. Surely it could not go any higher? 'Down to Mr Warrender for one thousand guineas,' and the gavel came down with a bang, and the colt was sold.

'I'm glad he's gone to David Warrender. He's gone to a good home.' Earl looked straight at her as he said it, repaying her for her help with reassurance that only he could give. His unexpected consideration took her unawares, and the anger died within her. She looked up into his face, relieved and grateful, and met there the same elusive, unreadable expression she had seen before. A look that made her suddenly uncertain of herself, uncertain of her anger that was her only defence against him, and robbed of it, she felt vulnerable, and afraid. Her eyes searched his face, questioning, pleading, and dropped at last in frustration because his expression was written in a language she could not read, and did not understand. Any more than she understood. . . . She swallowed, struck by a sudden thought. Had she misjudged Earl? Had his derogatory remark about racehorse owners been aimed at

Horace Blantyre, and not, as she thought, at herself? Had his sotto voce comment been conspiratorial, linking them together in a shared aversion instead of, as she believed, a barb aimed to wound her? Earl admitted spotting the man in the crowd two minutes before Steve spoke. Two minutes before he made the remark. And she had said. . . . Her eyes widened with dismay at the memory of what she had said to Earl. Her lips parted, trying silently to tell him she was sorry. She could not meet his look any longer, and her eyes faltered away, and turned back to Horace Blantyre.

'Avoid the points you would distrust in a man. . . .'

Bulging fat made Blantyre's tiny eyes seem even smaller than they were. His forehead sloped backwards at an alarming angle, and. . . . She gulped, and swung her eyes back to Earl, and discovered that instead of watching what was happening to his second yearling in the ring, he was watching her. Reading her thoughts. Sharing them, she saw, from the sudden flare of laughter in his eyes, knowing what was going through her mind and agreeing with it. His look teased her to laughter, dared her to release the chuckle of amusement that fought for its freedom and very nearly won. It formed a sudden bond between them of shared hilarity, almost making her feel grateful to Horace Blantyre for his part in forging the link, fragile though it might be, and a quick warmth flooded through her at the sharing, the first she had known with Earl.

'You might introduce me to your lady friend.'

'He sounds almost coy,' Roma thought disgustedly, and stopped her grimace of distaste in the nick of time.

'Meet Miss Forrester.' Earl sounded stiffly formal, as well as reluctant, Roma noticed with quick glee.

'We haven't exactly met, but. . . .' Horace Blantyre held out his hand, and Roma touched it briefly, and let his limp grip go with quick distaste. 'I recognise you, of course.'

'Recognise me?' She had never met the man before, she was certain of that. Even among the hundreds of passengers who had flown with the airline, she was sure she would have recognised him again. She had an excellent memory for faces.

'From your photograph in the racing pages of today's paper, of course.' Their unwelcome companion shook out his newspaper triumphantly. 'I must say, Paget,' he said with a sly look, 'you have excellent taste when it comes to choosing a filly for yourself.' He gave a high whinny of laughter at what he obviously considered to be an excellent joke, and Roma's temper snapped.

'The man's insufferable!' she told herself angrily. Owning a racehorse did not give him the right to apply his odious expressions to herself. She opened her mouth to tell him so, but Earl spoke first.

'I suggest, Blantyre——' he began, and his voice dripped ice.

'No suggestions necessary, old chap. The picture tells it all.' The man's chin wobbled when he laughed, Roma saw with disgust. 'See you in the bar later, eh?' And thrusting his opened newspaper into Earl's hands, he smirked at Roma and waddled off through the crowd.

The news sheets were folded so that the photograph lay on top. She hardly dared to look at it. She had to nerve herself not to cover her eyes with her hands, but they were drawn to the photograph as if by a magnet.

Herself, in Earl's arms. Strained to him in a close embrace, his mouth pressed down upon her own, locked in a lovers' kiss. The picture was a living lie. She pressed her hands to her lips, stifling a moan, unable to bear the lie, unable to bear the truth that lay behind it.

'The face of delight.' The caption mocked her. The reporter had misunderstood the import of her words. Earl's swift action had prevented her folly from being made public, and saved both himself and her from the consequences that would surely have followed. But need the reporter have given vent to his enthusiasm quite so freely? she asked herself bitterly.

'Earl Paget, owner of the Burdon Court stud and training stables, caught in an off-duty moment,' the writer burbled on. 'This afternoon, Mr Paget tasted victory at

Auteuil. Has he found another winner, off course?' it asked coyly.

If the reporter meant herself, he could not have been more mistaken, Roma thought wretchedly, and choked back a sob. Why did Horace Blantyre have to appear just at that moment, with his newspaper photograph? she asked herself in silent anguish. The frail, brittle moment when for the very first time she had found a bond with Earl. And now the moment lay trampled into the dust by the heavy-footed, insensitive reason for the bond. A timeless second of beauty, fallen and crushed, and out of the race before it had even reached its first hurdle.

CHAPTER EIGHT

EARL's face gave away nothing of what he was thinking. He looked down at the photograph for an endless, heartstopping minute, and then he looked up again, straight at Roma, and the strange, undefinable expression was gone from his eyes. They were hard, and unforgiving. Remembering. She began to tremble. It was as if a cold wind blew over her, through her, freezing away the laughter that had lain between them. She caught her breath, waiting for him to speak. Waiting for him to remind her what the photograph stood for, but all he said was,

'We needn't stay here any longer, now the two yearlings have been sold. Steve will attend to all the details.'

'Why don't we wait for Steve?' she asked quickly. She did not want to go back without Steve. She could not face the long journey back to Burdon Court with only the newspaper and its condemnatory photograph for company. She needed Steve, as a buffer between herself and Earl. She said desperately, 'If he came back with us, it would save him from having to bother with the train. It would save his fare. . . .' It would save her from having to face the forthcoming hours alone with Earl. 'It's only just after midday,' she protested, 'we've still got all the afternoon.'

'It's a long journey home, and it'll be dark by four o'clock,' he replied. 'By the time we've had lunch it'll be gone one o'clock.'

'Surely you're not afraid of driving in the dark?' she laughed scornfully, taunting him with being afraid, trying to drive him into waiting for the head lad. 'After all this sunshine, it'll stay light for longer tonight. You could wait for an hour or two, for Steve's convenience, there's no need to drag us away the second the sale is over,' she insisted.

'I'm dragging us away, as you put it, because I'll be dragging a horsebox behind the Range Rover,' he turned her words back on her impatiently. 'And after all this sunshine, we're likely to encounter fog on the way back. It's the first week in November, not the first week in June,' he reminded her cuttingly.

And they seemed to be manufacturing their own special brand of fireworks to throw at one another, Roma thought wretchedly. Out loud, she said reluctantly,

'It's up to you. You're driving.' Her expression made it plain that if she herself was behind the wheel, they would remain and take Steve back with them, her demeanour accusing him of lack of consideration towards the head lad. The benign warmth of the late sunshine accusing him of being over cautious.

'It *is* up to me, and we'll leave the moment we've finished lunch,' he told her decisively, and her lips tightened. Earl had the whip hand now, just as he had in France with the return flight tickets in his possession. She could not get back to Burdon Court without him. 'We'll go and eat,' he took her by the arm masterfully, and drew her away through the crowd. 'Would you like a drink first?'

'Not for me, thanks,' she refused. Horace Blantyre had said he would be in the bar, she had no doubt he would remain there until it closed, and she had no desire to bump into him again. 'Don't let me prevent you,' she grasped at the only straw left available to her.

'I never drink when I'm driving.' He instantly took the straw away, and steered her into the nearby grillroom, to the eating counter that at any other time she would have approached with a good appetite, drawn by the tempting aroma that drifted from the open grills at the back. He tossed the newspaper on to the counter. She did not know if he did it deliberately so that the photograph lay face upwards, confronting her. She could not blame him, because she had no proof. He drew up a stool for her to sit comfortably, and simultaneously gave their order across the counter and it came promptly from the sizzling array of steaks, and the paper lay where he had tossed it, untouched between them.

It pointed at her like an accusing finger, spoiling her enjoyment in the succulent meats that tasted like rags in her mouth, but through which she plodded her way stolidly, making the food last as long as possible, anything to delay the start of their return journey. Perhaps, she thought hopefully, if she could delay it for long enough, Earl might yet change his mind and wait for Steve. She asked for more salt, a different sauce, fidgeted with her coffee, then changed her mind and had tea instead, until Earl growled at her impatiently, recognising her tactics for what they were,

'Are you sure you wouldn't like to start all over again, and have something long and complicated, cooked for you from scratch?' he asked her bitingly. She did not want the meal she had got, and she prodded it round and round on her plate resentfully, and jumped when Steve spoke from just behind them.

'I thought I'd be too late to catch you.'

Roma dropped her fork with a clatter, and turned to him eagerly. Perhaps, after all, he was not going to the suppliers? Perhaps he had changed his mind?

'We should have started out an hour ago,' Earl said shortly, with a significant glance at Roma that brought angry colour to her face, but before she could think of a reply he asked Steve, 'Have you eaten?' thus refuting her earlier accusation of lack of consideration towards his head lad.

'I had my lunch early,' Steve replied. 'I've been offered a lift to the suppliers, so I ate while I had the chance, it'll give me an early start.'

'We could wait for you,' Roma pressed, but Steve shook his head,

'You'll need to be on your way,' he refused, and Roma felt a flash of irritation at the obsession that seemed to afflict Steve as well as Earl, of wanting an early start on the journey home. Surely the stable staff could cope for a few short hours without them? she thought sarcastically, they both acted as if they were indispensable. 'You can be half way home before I catch the train,' Steve sounded the knell on her hopes, and added, 'If I'm too late getting back tonight I won't disturb you, Guv'nor, I'll give you a report at the stables in the morning. Have a good journey,' he wished them, 'with a bit of luck you won't run into any fog. If you start out fairly soon, you'll be home shortly after dark.'

'If Roma's appetite allows us to start out soon.' Earl's eyes glinted, and Roma flushed angrily.

'I don't want any more.' She pushed her plate away. There was no point in trying to delay the start of their journey any longer, now that Steve was not coming back with them. She saw Earl glance at the contents of her plate, that for all her delaying tactics, she had scarcely touched. She tensed, waiting for him to say something about her wasted meal, ready for a sharp retort if he did. It was on the tip of her tongue to tell him she could not swallow a meal wholesale in a few minutes, which would have been unjustified since they had been in the grillroom for over an hour, but she did not care, she did not feel like being just to Earl at the moment. But all he said was,

'I'll give you exactly ten minutes, and no more,' when she paused at the door of the powder room on their way out. She joined him exactly five minutes later. There was no point in wasting any more time now, and he was waiting for her at the exit as she came out. Making sure I shan't run away, I suppose, she told herself critically. He need not have worried. She had no intention of making her own way back to Burdon Court without him. She did not even know where the nearest railway station was, and with Steve gone, she had no other guide. She noticed Earl was carrying a plastic shopping bag, which he had not had, she felt sure, when she left him. It looked incongruous dangling from his hand. She had seen him handling all sorts of implements, stable tools, harness, steering wheels, but never holding a plastic shopping bag before. It made him look curiously domesticated. It made her want to giggle, suddenly. She looked up at him, and the expression on his face took away her desire to giggle, and changed it into an urgent desire to cry.

'What on earth's the matter with me?' she asked herself desperately. Her normally stable emotions seemed to have completely deserted her, and those that had taken their place yo-yoed up and down between one extreme and the other in a manner that left her bewildered, and helpless to cope.

'Don't forget to fasten your seat belt.'

She fastened it. She would have liked to defy him, but found she had not got the strength. Being with Earl was a constant battle of wills, she discovered wearily, and she did not feel equal to a physical tussle as well. He would win anyway. She sank back into the seat, too tired to resist. She felt him look at her, keenly, probing her unexpected acquiescence, but he started the Range Rover without comment and they pulled away from her first experience of a yearling sales.

Earl was an accomplished driver. Mindful of the horsebox behind them he kept to a moderate pace, choosing to travel on the minor roads rather than use the motorway. A series of villages came and went, and unconsciously Roma relaxed, soothed by the flow of scenery. The vivid pageant of the dying year still stained trees and hedgerows with glorious colour, the late spell of good weather tempting the leaves to linger. As the afternoon progressed, children newly released from school scuffed happily through the bronze and yellow carpet, some of the older ones busily gathering sack loads of the fallen bounty to add fuel to their bonfires, which stood in conical splendour in almost every cottage garden along the way. For something to do, Roma began to count the bonfires.

'There were twelve in that village alone!' she exclaimed. She had not realised they were so close to the macabre yearly celebration. 'Which day is it?' She leaned forward automatically to check the date from the newspaper which lay half concealed under the plastic shopping bag on the parcel tray in front of her.

'Tomorrow's the fifth,' Earl said laconically.

'Will the stable lads have a bonfire?'

They slipped easily into conversation. Roma did not know how it happened, it just did. Without any warning, they were talking to one another easily, naturally, not using words as weapons any more but letting them flow smoothly, unbarbed between them. Guy Fawkes' Night had provided them with an unexpected neutral patch of ground on which they could both stand. Roma mentally blessed the unlamented Parliamentary reprobate, and asked lazily,

'Will the stable lads have a bonfire? A lot of them seem still young enough to enjoy fireworks.'

'Steve is releasing the four youngest to go to the village bonfire, so long as they're back by ten o'clock,' Earl answered. 'The others will be on duty, in shifts, all night.'

'They're not usually on duty like that, surely?' After evening stables she knew the lads went off for the evening, leaving the stables in charge of one lad and the evening patrol man with his guard dog. Because Earl lived on the premises there was no need for further staff after the horses were bedded down for the night, except in an emergency if one of the animals happened to be sick or injured.

'It's necessary, on Bonfire Night. I daren't take any risks, with a stable full of thoroughbreds. They're highly strung, and nervous. It only needs one irresponsible re-veller to get too close to the stables with a firecracker, and

DANGEROUS RAPTURE 105

one bang would be enough to cause chaos,' he said cryptically. 'I'd rather guard against it than have to deal with the consequences.'

'I didn't realise.' Her tone was defensive, her guard against him instinctively raised again. There was so much about Earl's world that she did not know, so much she had to learn. And if she learned it, of what use would it be to her? she wondered drearily, since she would never share in the world she was so eager to learn about.

'Why should you?' he asked her, uncritically. 'Airliners don't jump out of their skins if they hear a bang.'

'Airliners haven't got skins to jump out of.'

The laughter came back between them. Earl's teeth flashed white in a grin, and a chuckle bubbled from Roma's lips, spontaneous and merry, the first carefree sound she had made in Earl's presence since she came to Burdon Court. It brought the man's eyes fleetingly away from the road and on to her face, a piercing look that held once more the elusive quality she had tried so desperately to grasp and understand, and each time, failed. And now his look held a question as well, and she could not understand that either, so how was she supposed to answer?

'You won't see many individual bonfires in Down Burdon,' he commented, his eyes once more raking the road ahead, alert in concentration. 'Most of our stable staff live in the village, and they understand the need to keep the fireworks to a minimum, so I have their backing.'

'For what?' He was still talking in riddles, but she wanted him to keep on talking just the same. She wanted to remain on the neutral territory for as long as it would hold her, unwilling to leave it for the quagmire of uncertainty and antagonism that broke her heart, and wearied her spirit, and in which she had floundered ever since she met Earl.

'Burdon Court Stud and Training Stables subsidises the village bonfire,' Earl explained briefly, 'with the proviso that the fire itself is held at the other end of the village from where Burdon Court lies, and the fireworks purchased with the subsidy are those that don't go bang.'

'Little boys love bangers,' she protested.

'The little boys in Down Burdon nearly all have Burdon Court estate employees as their fathers, so they have to make do with Catherine wheels and sparklers instead,' he answered drily.

It was almost feudal. She stared at him for a disbelieving second.

'How typical!' she thought scathingly, the easy neutrality between them forgotten. Earl's high-handed assumption that, because he had a training stables in the vicinity, the whole village must defer to its needs. That he had the divine right to control not only the activities of his staff but of their families as well, even down to the children's fireworks. A spark of latent rebellion burst into bright flame inside her, and exploded like the fireworks that were at issue.

'That's monstrous!' she cried indignantly. She put aside the laws of common sense that told her the children were better off, and infinitely safer, with fireworks that did not explode. She closed her mind to the yearly horrific toll of maiming and even blinding that resulted from explosives falling into young and careless hands.

'It's a sensible precaution.' He slanted a look at her that denied her right to interfere.

'I've got every right,' she told herself passionately. 'While Silver Cloud remains in Earl's stables, I've got a stake in them, too. That gives me the right,' she justified herself. Aloud she cried angrily, 'It's a precaution that can't be necessary. The village is a long way from Burdon Court. It took me ages to walk between them, the day I arrived.' He was simply being over-cautious, she told herself scornfully, the same as he had been today by insisting on returning from the yearling sales so early. Over-cautious? Or merely showing his authority? Enjoying a sense of power?

'It's a long way between the Court and the village if you go by the lane,' Earl retorted, and his voice held a steely quality, 'but sound travels direct. The lane curves, following the course of the river, and bends back in a U-turn to reach the village. The cottages at the one end of the village, the end nearest to the stables,' he emphasised, 'lie just on the other side of the park land which marks the Burdon Court boundary. They're much too near for comfort if the families decide to each have a bonfire, and start setting off rockets which might easily fly towards the stables.'

The laughter had fled, and the antagonism was back between them again, like a barbed wire fence, waiting to rend her if she ventured too close.

'There's nothing to prevent you from going to the village bonfire if you feel so inclined.' His tone said he did not care either way, and she flinched away from its hard uncaring.

It would have been nice, she thought wistfully, if she could have gone to the village bonfire with Earl. If he had said—oh, impossible dream!—if he had said, 'Come with me,' she would have gone eagerly, joyfully, even though she did not like fireworks herself, had never liked them, and avoided them whenever possible. But Earl would be on duty as well as his stable staff tomorrow night, she knew him well enough by now to be aware that he did not ask of his staff what he was not prepared to do himself, so it was no use wishing. . . .

'I don't like fireworks.'

There were more than enough of the verbal variety between herself and Earl to satisfy even an enthusiast, she thought ruefully, and lapsed into silence, mourning the transient moments of camaraderie that had flown, and taken along with them the laughter and the sunshine. She watched with despondent eyes as the early dusk outside the Range Rover windscreen dulled the bright colours and settled in a uniform grey across the barren winter fields, matching her mood. Even the windscreen seemed to cloud in front of her, as if trying to close her in, alone and groping through the fog of her own bewilderment and misery.

'Fog . . .?'

She sat upright, her mind startled into clarity at the

same moment that Earl flicked the windscreen wipers into action with a muttered ejaculation.

'What . . .?'

'Fog,' he confirmed curtly.

'It's only mist.' She relaxed, relieved, as the windscreen wipers cleared the haze from the glass, and the world appeared again, if not too clearly, at least with good enough visibility in which to drive with care.

'It'll thicken,' Earl predicted.

'Don't be a pessimist,' she said sharply. 'We're travelling close to a river,' she pointed out of her side window to where a wide waterway flowed through a valley some distance below the road. 'The mist follows the water, I expect. It normally does, and once the road leaves the river, we'll be clear of the haze.'

'It's more than just a haze,' he pointed out bluntly, 'and the road doesn't leave the river, unfortunately. It drops down into the valley, and follows beside it for the next five or six miles, with the river on the one side, and water fields on the other. If there's going to be a fog, it always lies along this stretch.'

'Then why did you come this way?' she turned on him impatiently. 'Surely there'a another road you could have chosen?'

'There is,' he retorted, and his tone matched her own for sharpness. 'The other road takes us over fifty miles out of our way, and I saw no reason to use it when this route is perfectly adequate. By starting out early enough, it's possible to get through the river stretch in broad daylight, and avoid any chance of fog rising with the darkness. If you hadn't taken such an age over your lunch. . . .' he began critically, and Roma's temper snapped.

'That's right, blame me,' she cried angrily. 'How like a man! Whatever happens, it's never a man's fault,' she said bitterly, and thrust aside her guilt at being the cause of the delay. An extra hour on the road would have been time enough to take them right away from the low-lying ground beside the river long before it had time to get dark.

'It's Earl's fault, just as much as mine,' she excused herself mutinously. 'He should have explained to me his reason for wanting to come away early. How was I to know their reason, if they didn't explain?' Neither Earl nor Steve had thought it necessary to explain. With typical male arrogance, they thought that it was sufficient for them to say what it was they wanted, and expect everyone else to fall in with their plans without question. 'Well, I won't,' she fumed, 'and it's high time Earl realised that.' The thickening mist outside the window told her that Earl must already know, and blame her for her stubbornness, and would no doubt make her regret it later. Even if the fog did not make her regret it very soon. She stared about her with growing apprehension.

They had followed the river for miles, losing it for a while as it looped and turned, flirting with the road, then closing in on it again. An hour ago, its waters gleamed clear and bright under the sunshine. Now she stared downwards through the side window with anxious eyes, now the water was no longer visible. Instead of the river, all she could see was a long white cottonwool pillow of mist, heaving and rolling above the water, blotting out the valley into which even now the road inexorably descended. She twisted round in her seat and faced Earl.

'Turn back!' she cried shrilly. 'Turn. . . .'

'There's no point.' He switched on the headlights and kept going, and Roma felt an urgent desire to shake him.

'We can't just drive straight down into the fog,' she gasped. 'It's madness!' He must have taken leave of his senses, she told herself furiously. If he was simply trying to frighten her, to pay her back for being the cause of the delay, he was succeeding beyond his wildest expectations. A thrill of pure fear shivered through her as Earl slowed the vehicle to a crawl, and the nose dipped sharply downwards, over the crest of the rise they had just climbed, and into the mist-filled valley below them. The claustrophobic whiteness rose to meet them, enveloped them. Roma felt stifled, trapped. It pressed against the side windows, against the windscreen. She could not see. She felt she could not breathe.

'I'm getting out.' She turned swiftly and reached for the door handle.

'Stay where you are.' Quick as lightning, Earl grabbed her and pulled her hand away.

'I can't . . . I won't. . . .' she panted, and tried to twist herself free from his hold. She might as well have tried to push against steel bars. His fingers gripped her wrist with Herculean strength, and she sobbed as she fought to free herself.

'Let me go . . . turn back. . . .'

'I can't turn back, it isn't safe.'

'Do you call this safe?' she cried hysterically. 'We could go over the edge of the road, and roll into the river.'

'Be still for a minute, and listen to me!' With an angry tug, he pulled on the brake and stopped the Range Rover in its tracks, and grabbing her by the shoulders with both hands, he gave her a hard shake.

'We can't turn round,' he told her brusquely, when she gasped into shuddering silence. 'The road's too narrow to turn, and I can't back the whole outfit up over the hill again, the fog will be just as bad in the dip on the other side, and it's risking an accident if there's another vehicle following behind us.'

'We could park here.'

'It isn't safe,' he insisted, 'we're only just beyond a sharp bend, and still too close to the crest of the hill. It would be dangerous to park here even in broad daylight, let alone in these conditions. I'm making for a layby about fifty or so yards downhill. We can pull in there, off the road, and sit it out until the fog clears.'

'That might be all night!' she gasped, horror-struck. 'We can't stay here all night. I won't. . . .'

'You can get out and walk if you want to, I'm going to park up.' Uncompromisingly Earl presented her with a choice that was really no choice at all.

'But. . . .' she began again, desperately.

'There aren't any "buts",' he interrupted her grimly.

'If you want to try and grope your way through that,' he waved an eloquent hand at the opaque air outside the windscreen, 'you're more than welcome.'

'We might have to wait until daylight comes,' she realised in a small voice. What would people think if they were out all night? The question she dared not voice raced round and round in her mind, and found no answer, only the grey blanket of fog pressing against the windows, which in itself was as uncompromising as the trainer. What would the staff at Burdon Court think? The housekeeper? She strained her eyes, trying to pierce the gloom by sheer willpower, but she could not see the end of the Range Rover bonnet, let alone the road beyond it.

'It's more than likely we'll be stuck here until daylight,' he gave her no comfort. 'And if we are, it'll give you time to reflect on the success of your delaying tactics at lunchtime.' He slanted her an angry glance. 'Now sit still, and don't try any more crazy tricks like trying to jump out on to the road,' he warned her, 'do you understand?' His grip on her shoulders tightened, stressing his order.

'I won't.' She nodded numbly, and he gave her a long, hard look, then his fingers loosed their grip and his hands left her shoulders, satisfied that for the moment at least she would obey him, and she longed to clasp his hands and draw them back to her again, and beg him to hold her, because while he held her she felt safe, no matter what the danger from the fog and the river and the risk of being run into from another vehicle coming behind.

'Earl. . . .' she whispered, and choked back a sob because he did not hear her. His head was thrust through the window on his side of the vehicle, his eyes raking the route ahead, probing the fog for a familiar bush, or tree, guiding them more by instinct than by sight.

'Open your side window, and watch out for me on that side.' His sudden order made her jump, but she did as he told her, and opened the window with trembling fingers that felt as if they had not the strength to move the glass. 'Look for a sign on the roadside. It's a long, oblong thing, and the headlights should pick it up even in these conditions, the words are pricked out in cats' eyes.'

'What does it say?'

What did it matter what it said? she asked herself hysterically. What did anything matter, but that they should come through the fog safely? Bitterly, now, she blamed herself for being the cause of the danger. The cause of danger to Earl.

'It says "layby",' he said briefly.

Roma thrust her head through the window, and the fog reached out and clung to her face, icily cold on her cheeks, her forehead, beading her hair with tiny wet droplets, clammily threatening. She could not see a thing. Desperately she strained her eyes, trying to force them to see, making them ache with the effort, that was useless because there was nothing there except the all-enveloping fog. No tree. No bush. No sign that said 'layby'. Nothing but the darkness, and the fog. Numbly she realised that it was quite dark now. The darkness seemed to accuse her, condemn her.

'The sign—it's here. The sign's here!' She drew her head back into the cab, and bumped her chin on the door ledge in her excitement. 'I've found it.' She wanted to shout aloud to the world that she had found the sign for Earl. 'It's here!' she cried jubilantly.

'Fine,' he answered laconically, and allowed the Range Rover to roll straight past it.

'Why don't you turn in? You said you'd turn into the layby?' She stared at him, nonplussed. If this was his idea of a joke, to ask her to stick her head through an open car window and get half choked, and frozen by fog, looking for a sign he did not want in the first place, she did not think it was funny, she told herself furiously. 'You said you wanted. . . .'

'And so I did,' he replied crisply. 'But I can't do a right angle turn while I'm towing a horsebox behind me, it's too long. I've got to allow room for the tow to come into the layby, as well as the Range Rover.'

She had forgotten they were towing the horsebox. 'Don't get too near to the edge,' she warned him fearfully.

Although the road started to dip away from the crest of the hill, they were still nowhere near the bottom, and the long drop down into the valley and the river below haunted her imagination.

'Can you see a post and rail fence on your side?' asked Earl.

'No.'

'Then we're nowhere near the edge,' he told her briefly. 'This layby was specially built and levelled so that people could pull off the road to look at the view without getting in the way of other traffic,' he added, and his lips twisted wryly at the irony of it. 'It's worth looking at, when the view's visible,' he said drily in answer to Roma's startled look. 'It looks as if we're here for a long stay, so I'll chock the wheels, just in case,' and he opened the driving door and swung to the ground.

'Earl, don't leave me!' She raised her voice in panic as he disappeared from her sight.

'Stay where you are, I shan't be long.' His face reappeared through the gloom, and his eyes were stern. 'Don't get any silly ideas about following me,' he warned her. 'I don't want to have to grope around in this murk, trying to find you. And remember, if you do feel an urge to go exploring, *you* could go over the edge, as well as the vehicle. And it's a long, steep drop.' He clipped his mouth shut on his parting shot, slammed the door behind him, and disappeared.

Even his footsteps made no sound, or if they did, it was muffled by the fog. It was as if he had vanished into another world. The silence was complete. It washed round her, total and unnerving. Although it was comfortably warm in the cab, she began to shiver uncontrollably. After what seemed a lifetime of waiting, she felt a movement towards the rear of the Range Rover, and it was followed immediately by a muffled clatter. She tensed, her nerves taut, waiting for the crash. Had another vehicle followed them into the layby, and not seen them in time? Had it run into the horsebox, which in turn would run into the Range Rover? Had it—unbearable thought—had it run into Earl? She clenched her teeth, waiting for the crash, waiting for his cry. Instead, a cheerful whistle travelled back along the side of the Range Rover, approaching the cab.

'California, here I come. . . .' It seemed to be the theme song of the stables. An hysterical desire to laugh took possession of her, and she suppressed it with difficulty as Earl jackknifed himself back behind the wheel again and shut the door on the fog with a decisive slam, and said, matter-of-factly,

'Now we can eat.'

'What was the clatter?' She had to know.

'Only me, putting down the back of the horsebox to get at the chocks.' He reached across to the parcel tray and fished out the plastic shopping bag, and tipped it up to reveal two substantial packets of sandwiches. 'Tuck in,' he advised her, and dropped one of the packets on to her lap. She stared at it as if mesmerised, and the desire to laugh drained out of her.

Food! He had brought food with him. Plenty of it. Enough for them both, if they had to remain out all night.

'You planned this!' Roma turned on him stormily. 'You deliberately planned to strand us here all night!' She faced him like a cornered wild thing, knowing itself to be trapped. 'You knew,' she accused him hotly.

'I knew that you'd only eaten a couple of mouthfuls of an excellent lunch, and taken over an hour to do it,' he refuted her accusation, tight-faced, his eyes as angry as her own. 'I knew that we faced a long journey home, and by all the laws of nature you'd be practically starving before we got back. I knew I didn't want to waste time on the journey home, stopping to get you another meal.' His voice was harsh, throwing the blame back on to her shoulders for their present difficulty. 'As it turns out, you can take all the time you want to, over this meal,' he thrust at her bitingly, and dropped a plastic dispensing beaker of fruit juice in her lap. 'Here's something to wash the sandwiches down with.'

She needed the drink. The food seemed to stick in her throat, even though she acknowledged herself to be ravenous.

'What will they think when we don't turn up at Burdon Court? We might be here until the morning.' Her voice choked into silence at the possibility.

'What can they think, except that we started out later than we should have done, and were caught by the fog?' Earl's eyes glared into hers, angry, challenging, daring her to put into words what she feared people might think.

She did not dare. She could not bring herself to say them. Instead, she bit into a sandwich she did not want, and feared it would choke her if she tried to swallow, so that she had to press the top off the plastic beaker, and take a hasty drink.

'If you've finished, we might as well turn in. The fog won't lift now, before sun-up tomorrow.'

'Turn in?' There was nowhere to turn in to. And in any case. . . . She swallowed, and stared up at him, and fear and uncertainty sparked off the ready anger that was her only defence against him. 'Turn in—where to?' She did not dare to say, 'who with?'

'In the horsebox, of course.' He glanced at her impatiently. 'Where else?'

'I'm not sleeping in a horsebox,' she began indignantly.

'Please yourself,' he snapped, and his eyes were like gimlets, boring into her's. 'It's spotlessly clean, and there are clean horse blankets we can use for bedding. You can sit up and catnap through the night if you want to. I want a good night's sleep, I've got a busy day ahead of me tomorrow.' With a swift movement he thrust open the door of the Range Rover and swung out.

'Earl, don't leave me. . . .'

'Then don't be so stubborn,' he growled. 'Come with me . . . oh,' his eyes raked her face, took in her white cheeks and her apprehensive eyes, 'if it's the proprieties you're worried about, you needn't,' he assured her with a sarcastic inflection in his voice that brought a scarlet flush across the whiteness. 'The horsebox is a double one, there's a partition right along the centre. We'll be in separate cubicles,' he taunted her.

'I didn't mean . . . I wasn't suggesting. . . .' Roma stammered to a confused halt. She did not know what she meant, or what she suggested. She only knew that she did not want to be left alone in the Range Rover for the rest of the night. Left alone without Earl. Hurriedly she slid across under the driving wheel and wriggled to the ground. In her haste not to be left behind, she collided with Earl, stumbling into him, and would have tripped and fallen if he had not caught and held her.

'I didn't mean . . . I was only going to. . . .' she started breathlessly, her face upraised to his.

'To say goodnight?' Earl suggested mockingly as her voice trailed into silence. His arms tightened around her, imprisoning her, drawing her close against him so that she could not move. 'What a good idea,' he murmured, and bent his head above her.

His kiss mocked her, light, challenging, deliberately provocative, seeking to draw a response from her, and because it succeeded so easily, it made her angry, and she started to struggle in his arms. And then, without warning, his kiss suddenly changed. It was as if her panting resistance set ablaze a smouldering fire within him. His lips ceased to play with her own, and became hungry, demanding. A shock like an electric charge thrilled through her as their lips touched. It reminded her of a storm she had once experienced, she thought bemusedly. It started as a playful wind, buffeting and teasing, annoying but bearable, and the next second it turned into a raging storm that shattered her resistance, laughed at her puny struggles, and battered her defences, so that, weak and helpless, she had no defences left, and no strength to struggle any more.

The pressure of his arms increased, straining her to him, but she no longer wanted to be free. His lips pressed down upon her own with a cruel force, bruising, painful, but with a tiny inarticulate sound Roma turned her face up to his, glorying in the pain. Her heart throbbed with a

wild, abandoned beat that set the blood racing through
her veins, rousing a slumbering passion such as she had
never known before. She felt her temples throb with the
force of it, like the drumbeat of racing hooves. It claimed
her breath and her senses, so that she swayed, half fainting, in his arms, which tightened round her further still,
holding her up, making the fog, and the steep drop into
the river below, and the world they had left and the one
to which, when daylight came again, they must return,
alike vanish from her consciousness, and left her in a world
filled only with,

'Earl,' she moaned softly, and surrendered to his arms.

CHAPTER NINE

SOMETHING tickled her ear. She tried to raise her hands to
flick it away, and discovered they were enveloped in
something soft, and warm, and smelling faintly with the
sweet, slightly musty smell of clean wool. She thrust
against the warm softness, and the horse blanket fell away
from her and she sat up abruptly, memory flooding back.

Memory of Earl's kiss. Roma's eyes glowed as she re
membered, and her fingers raised to tenderly touch her
lips where they had been touched by his. She wriggled
into a more comfortable position and leaned back against
the partition that divided the horsebox into two, the high
wooden wall that separated her from Earl, and gave herself up to remembering, to living again their parting of
the night before.

'Enough of this,' he said in a hoarse voice. He raised
his head, and his hands on each side of her face tore their
lips apart. She whimpered at the agony of the separation,
but he was not to be moved.

'You're getting frozen in this fog,' he said in a rough
voice.

What did she care about the fog, when her mind and

body glowed with an inward fire that warmed her through
and through, a dormant fire that had smouldered all these
years, waiting for Earl to fan it into flame?

'I'll unhook the blankets from off the box walls.' He
reached up and took one off the side wall, and one off the
middle partition, long brown horse blankets that were as
soft as those on her own bed, and only differed in the
colour. 'Now come to me,' he bade her. She came to him,
stepping trembling up to him, staring up into his face,
and her eyes were soft, and her lips parted expectantly.
Earl paused, the blanket held high in his hands, and
looked down into her eyes, a long, lingering look that
seemed to probe into the very secret regions of her heart.
And then he said abruptly, closing her lips, and banishing
the softness from her eyes by the curtness of his tone,

'Stand still, and let me roll this blanket round you.'

He rolled her into a cocoon of woollen warmth, but it
was not the warmth she longed for. Not the blissful, safe
warmth of his arms. She quivered under his touch, and
raised her face beseechingly to his.

'You're cold.' He misunderstood her trembling. 'I
shouldn't have kept you outside in the fog for so long.'

A million years would not have been too long for her,
thought Roma distractedly. She would have stood with
him in a snowdrift, and not have felt the cold, but
cocooned in the blanket she could not move, she could
only let her eyes speak for her the words her voice failed
to utter. Imploring him for one more kiss. . . . She could
not know how appealing she looked, her dark cap of hair
faintly pearled with dampness from the fog, her eyes wide
like still grey pools, her face a fragile flower in the dark
folds of the blanket. The man's eyes glowed with a strange
light as he looked down on her, the same light she had
seen in them before, and could not interpret.

'Earl?' The question was a whisper.

'You're getting cold.' His voice was hoarse. Perhaps it
was the fog affecting his throat? Swiftly he bent and
touched the tip of her nose tantalisingly with his lips, then
he stooped and lifted her off her feet and gathered her,

blanket and all, high into his arms, and stepped into the horsebox.

'If you need me, just bang on the partition,' he told her, and laid her down in the narrow cubicle and covered her over with the other blanket, tucking it round her to keep out the draughts. 'There's no need to be nervous, the Range Rover can't roll. The brakes are on, and I've fixed chocks under the wheels of the horsebox.'

How could she be nervous, with Earl so close to her, on the other side of the partition? And as for needing him. . . . Every fibre of her being cried out with her need of him, aching for him, yearning for him, would go on needing and yearning for all the rest of her days.

'Now sleep,' he commanded her, 'you've had a long day.' She had been up since five o'clock that morning, and Earl, she knew, had been up long before that, but she felt no desire to sleep. The feel of his lips still burned upon her own, and trailed fire across her throat and cheeks, and the feel of his arms straining her to him, armoured her against tiredness, so that she lay wide-eyed in the darkness, her ears alert for the sound of his every movement on the other side of the wooden partition.

The trailer rocked as he unhooked the rugs from off the walls. She could almost follow his movements as he rolled himself in one blanket, and the trailer rocked again as he lay down and pulled the other one over him, covering himself warmly as he had covered her. Roma inched nearer to the partition until her cheek touched the wood, so close to Earl and yet so far apart, and wondered how she could bear the long dark hours until the daylight came again, and they could once more be together.

Even a yearning heart must find some rest, and Nature's balm stole upon her unawares, spiriting away the tensions and the bewilderment, the anger and the heartache, and when she roused and opened her eyes it was to the consciousness of growing daylight, and the corner of the blanket tickling her ear. Her wrist watch confirmed that it was nearly seven o'clock.

'Earl?' She scrambled to her feet, and grabbed at the

partition as the trailer rocked to her movement.

'Leave your blankets where they are, I'll hook them back on to the walls.'

Earl's face appeared round the end of the trailer. He looked fresh and clear-eyed, as if he had spent the night in his own bed at Burdon Court instead of in a bare wooden horsebox parked at the roadside. He reached in towards her as she made her unsteady way out of the narrow cubicle, afraid of setting the trailer rocking again.

'Hold on to me.' He grasped her round her waist and lifted her down on to the ground beside him, and she tilted her face up towards him, the memory of the night before still enfolding her with a warmth more penetrating than any blanket, soft in her shining eyes, and the silent invitation of her upraised lips.

'I'll give you ten minutes to stretch your legs before we start off,' he said briskly, refusing the invitation, and she stepped backwards as if he had struck her, anger and humiliation staining her cheeks with flaming colour. He made no move to stop her, he scarcely glanced at her as he stepped up into the trailer and reached for the horse blankets, and started to hook them back on to the wooden walls. 'You'll want this, I expect.' He picked up her shoulder bag and swung it towards her by the strap. 'There's a small waterfall where a stream comes down the rock, just a few yards along the road, if you want a wash,' he told her cheerfully. 'It's cold,' he warned.

The rosy glow of last night faded under the first douche of icy water against her cheeks. It shocked her back to early morning reality, to Earl's lack of caring, and a journey to be completed, and perhaps questions to be answered at the end of it. What would Steve think of their overnight absence? And Earl's housekeeper? Unanswered questions returned to torment her, and she completed a hurried toilet, and rejoined him at the Range Rover in well under the stipulated ten minutes.

'You might as well have a look at the view, now that it's visible,' he commented, and turned her by the shoulders to look out across the valley at their feet. The rising

sun painted the sky with a brief glory, turning the last
trailing wisps of river mist into pink gossamer, which dispersed even as she watched, and faded into nothingness,
like the colours in the clouds. It left behind only the cold,
grey light of an early November morning, a steely cold
that entered her heart and numbed her mind, and took
away the last of the blissful euphoria as Earl dropped his
hands from her shoulders and said practically,

'We'll be on our way now.' He helped her up into the
cab of the Range Rover, and slid behind the wheel himself. 'There's some sandwiches left, if you're hungry, and
a carton of fruit juice.'

She reached for the sandwiches, not because she wanted
them, but because they gave her something on which to
focus her eyes, so blurred she had difficulty in making out
which end of the package was which. Her fingers
trembled, fumbling with the wrapper, bringing Earl's eyes
briefly on to what she was trying to do.

'You'll have to fight your way through the wrapping,'
he predicted cheerfully, 'but at least it keeps the food
moist.' He made no move to help her. With a quick flick
he keyed the engine into life, and turned the Range Rover
and the trailer back on to the road, and left her to cope
with the difficulty herself.

A wave of anger surged through Roma at his total indifference; at the stubborn sandwich packet. The anger
cleared her vision, and rescued her pride, and she gave a
mighty tug that tore the wrapping apart and spilled the
sandwiches on to her lap, and drew an amused chuckle
from Earl that made her long to throw the sandwiches
and their packet at him, to punish him for his lack of
caring, for callously using his kisses to enliven a long, fog-
bound night, tempting her to bare her heart and reveal to
him her feelings that she did not want to acknowledge,
even to herself, and when she did he cruelly thrust them
back at her, unwanted. Her pride curled away from the
memory of her eager response, her naïve trust in him.

'Never again,' she vowed to herself silently. Earl used
his caresses to punish and humiliate, to satisfy himself,

without regard to her feelings. 'He's done it for the
last time,' she told herself staunchly, and blamed a non-
existent speck of grit for the tears that flooded her eyes.
She blinked them clear, and saw,

'Down Burdon?' Lost in her own unhappy reflections,
Roma had not realised they were so close to the end of
their journey. Familiar cottages passed the windows of
the Range Rover. A woman waved a greeting to them
from a front garden gay with late dahlias, and the small
boy she was seeing off to school turned towards them, but
he did not wave. Roma recognised the bright hair under
the sober uniform cap as belonging to the young apple
scrumper from the Lodge garden.

'Lord of the manor, waving to the cottagers,' she
sneered to herself as Earl returned the greeting with a
cheery lift of his hand. She was being unjust, but she did
not care, it helped to armour her against the trainer, and
served as a balm to her still raw pride.

'What are you pulling up for?' she asked him sharply.
Surely he did not intend to go back and complain to the
mother about the child scrumping a few scrubby apples?

'The string's coming towards us from the stables. It's
exercise time,' he answered casually, and added, 'I'll pull
in here and give them room to pass—the lane's a bit
narrow if another vehicle happens to come round the
bend.' He drew to a halt on the inside curve of the lane,
and sat watching the oncoming horses walking quietly in
line. Bob, the apprentice jockey, headed the string, riding
Silver Cloud. The filly looked superb, and Roma felt a
thrill of pride run through her as she watched the grey.
The horse was in perfect condition, ears pricked forward
and head proudly alert, obviously enjoying its morning
outing.

'She's mine!' Roma breathed to herself. She still found
it difficult to believe that the grey really belonged to her.
She ran her eyes along the string of horses, automatically
counting them. There were twelve in all, the first of the
two batches to exercise from the stables. There were three
or four fillies in front, then a couple of older, more sober

animals; Earl's own chestnut gelding was one. The rest were the colts she had seen before, they were the ones among which she ran when she chased the kitten.

This must be the same string, she realised. They were obviously the first out at exercise each morning in the routine of the stables. She turned her eyes away hastily from the bunch of colts at the back, and returned them to Silver Cloud, her pride.

She caught sight of a flash of carroty hair behind the hedge, at the same time as the firework soared over the tangle of twigs and landed with a hissing splutter of sparks, right under the hooves of the leading horses.

'It's a jumping jack!' she saw, horrified, and her hands rose instinctively to cover her ears as, true to its name, the firework gave a loud bang, jumped up into the air, and banged again as it landed, farther along the line of horses. At the second bang, pandemonium broke loose among the string. Earl wrenched open the driving door of the Range Rover with a muttered exclamation, and was out of the vehicle and running towards them before the firework had time to explode for the third time, and without giving herself time to think, Roma followed him. What she hoped to achieve, she had no clear idea, but she followed Earl just the same.

'Whoa!'

'Hold up, there!'

'Whoa!'

The desperate injunctions of the stable lads fell on deaf ears. The firecracker hissed and sparked and banged and jumped along the line of horses, as if drawn by some evil hand, and the orderly procession broke up in a mad panic. What had seconds before been a group of docilely walking horses turned into a wild-eyed, snorting, rearing mêlée of animals fighting their riders for their bits, intent only on bolting away from a succession of nerve-racking explosions that must have sounded like gunshots under their hooves. The black colt was the first to unship its jockey. With a shrill scream it bucked so hard that it seemed to stand on its head, and the boy described a perfect arc through the

air and landed in the middle of a nearby bramble thicket
with an outburst of imprecations that spoke eloquently of
the efficacy of its thorns, and at any other time would
have earned him a sharp rebuke from Earl. At any other
time, in a slow motion cartoon for instance, the scene
being enacted before her eyes might have seemed funny.
Roma did not feel like laughing now. It would have
needed a rodeo rider to have remained seated on the
panic-stricken mounts, as one after another the colts
followed the black's example, and bucked off their riders.
Stable boys seemed to pop out of their saddles in all
directions, and she watched with horrified eyes as Silver
Cloud reared, and went over on her back. She lost sight
of Bob, and felt sick at the possibility that the boy might
be pinned under the struggling horse, that lashed out with
all four hooves as it fought to regain its feet, and bolt
away from the exploding firework. Earl raced towards the
grey.

'Earl, be careful!'

He half turned, as if he realised for the first time that
she was following behind him.

'Go back!' he shouted at her urgently. 'Go back to the
car!' He broke off as a shrill whinny, an urgent cry,
'Behind you, Gov'nor!' and a wild clatter of hooves
brought him round again to face the string.

'Get down, Roma! Lie down!'

Even as he shouted, Earl turned with the agility of a
dancer, spinning on the balls of his feet as a big bay colt,
fully sixteen hands high, and looking to Roma's terrified
eyes as tall as a block of flats, got the bit between its
teeth, ridded itself of its struggling rider, and bolted
straight towards them.

'Lie down!'

Lie down, in the path of a bolting horse? Had Earl
gone crazy? It was as good as inviting her to get herself
killed. The thing to do was to run, as fast and as far away
as she possibly could, out of the animal's path. Out of
danger. But her feet would not obey her desperate order
to run. They seemed to be glued to the surface of the

lane, frozen into immobility with sheer terror. The horse came towards her with what seemed like the speed of an express train, and Roma stared at it, transfixed.

'Lie down!' Earl roared again, but this time he did not wait to see if she would obey him. He hurled himself straight at her with a perfectly aimed rugby tackle that took her under the knees, and felled her to the ground with a crash that knocked all the breath from her lungs, and awoke her mind from its frozen paralysis.

'Get up,' she cried. 'Get away! We'll both be killed!' She thrust at him with terrified hands, trying to push him from off her.

'Lie still, it's our only chance.'

He lay across her, his body sheltering her, his weight holding her down, and his hands remorselessly holding her still, stopping her frantic struggles to be free.

'We'll be killed,' she sobbed wildly. Nothing could save them. They lay directly in the path of the fear-crazed animal. She could feel the vibrations of its hooves pounding into her through the surface of the lane, a drum roll of destruction that beat through her mind in a tattoo of inevitable disaster. She shuddered, and turned her face into Earl's jacket as the colt raced up to them, a yard away, half a yard. . . .

With only inches to spare, the animal rose into the air in a perfectly timed jump that took it clear across them as if they were a hurdle on a racecourse, and it landed with feet to spare on the other side of them. They were safe! A wave of faintness made the world swim in a giddy circle round her, and Roma let herself thankfully go limp on the blessed security of the lane, but Earl gave her no respite. He took a quick look behind him to make sure that none of the other colts followed the bay's lead, then he swung to his feet and pulled her unceremoniously up with him.

'Are you hurt?' he asked her abruptly, and when she shook her head, incapable of coherent speech, he ordered her curtly, 'Go and sit in the Range Rover, where you'll be safe.' What he really meant, she thought resentfully, was where she would be out of his way, but she felt too dazed to argue, to do anything but lean against the hard metal side of the vehicle and watch silently as he hastened over to Bob. She saw with relief that the apprentice jockey was back on his feet, apparently unhurt, and struggling to hold the restless grey.

'Are you hurt?' She heard him repeat his question to the boy, who replied breathlessly,

'No, I'm all right, Guv'nor, but I don't think Willy is.'

The young rider of the bay colt sat limply on the grass verge, and Earl hurried over to him. Roma's faintness vanished. Years of independent coping came to her aid, and her mind cleared as if by magic. 'Earl can say what he likes,' she muttered to herself mutinously, and sped to join him beside the boy. 'Let me help, I'm trained in first aid.' She bent over Willy. 'Do you feel pain anywhere?' The boy was conscious, but seemed dazed.

'No, miss, only my wrist. I landed on my arm,' he groaned.

'Let me have a look.' The boy's arm was badly grazed from brutal contact with the hard surface of the lane, but there were no obvious signs of a fracture. 'Let's tie this round you to hold it, just in case.' She whipped off her own silk square and turned it into an impromptu sling. 'I'll take him back to the Range Rover with me,' she decided, and her look defied Earl to challenge her decision. To her surprise he merely nodded, and said,

'Go ahead, I'll go and collect Sean if you'll look after Willy.'

He accepted her help without hesitation, and she despised herself for the warm glow that coursed through her because this time, for the very first time, she was not simply a looker-on. For the moment of the emergency, she belonged. She put her arm around Willy's thin shoulders and helped him towards the Range Rover, while Earl hastened to where loud lamentations still echoed from the bramble thicket as the luckless lad tried to extricate himself from its clinging thorns.

'Sean sounds as if he's getting pretty badly scratched.'

Willy managed a puckish grin that Roma found greatly reassuring, and she helped him up into the high vehicle and belted him in.

'We'll take you to hospital and have your wrist X-rayed.'

'I don't want to go to no hospital, miss.' Alarm showed clear on the stable lad's white face. 'It'll mend on its own.'

'You'll both go for a check-up,' Earl returned with the other lad and glanced across his head at Roma. 'Sean's badly scratched, but he's not broken anything. Fortunately it's a stable rule that they all have anti-tetanus injections, so they're well protected.'

'Land sakes, Mr Paget! What on earth's going on?' The woman Roma saw at the cottage gate panted up to them, and her eyes widened in horror as they lit on Earl and the stable lad, both of whom bore faces and hands liberally torn and bleeding from their encounter with the bramble thicket. 'I was just going indoors when I saw that big bay colt come bolting past, with no rider on its back, only a few minutes since.'

'Your young Jimmy threw a firework under the feet of the string,' Sean snarled in a voice as barbed as the thorns he had just escaped.

'He never did? Eh, the little limb!' his mother exclaimed. 'I'm that sorry, Mr Paget. His dad'll kill him for this. . . .'

'Never mind how it happened now, Mrs Wright.' Earl cut across her protestations. 'We'll deal with Jimmy later. In the meantime, I need your help.'

'I'll do anything you say, Mr Paget,' the woman promised, eager to make amends for her delinquent son.

'Go and telephone your husband at the stables,' Earl instructed her. 'Ask him to ring the police and warn them to look out for the bay colt, and then to bring reinforcements here to help the lads walk the string back home. I don't want them ridden until they've quietened down. After that, tell Dave to take a couple of the lads and go in search of the bay colt. In the meantime I'll take these two boys to get some medical attention. I'll unhitch the trailer first,' he told Roma, 'we'll make better time that way.' He suited action to his words, freed the Range Rover from its tow, and leaving Roma in charge of the two casualties he hurried over to where the rest of the stable lads were busily occupied in trying to soothe their nervous charges. Roma marvelled at his gentleness with the highly strung animals, the unhurried patience with which he lent his strength to a stable lad here, his firmness with an animal there, drawing order out of chaos. Two of the horses he tied to a nearby tree, and set their stable lads one at each end of the line, to guard against oncoming traffic.

'Dave Wright will be with you in under ten minutes,' he told them, 'wait for him to come with help before you start to walk the string back to the stables.' He returned to the Range Rover and cautiously keyed the engine into life, rolling it gently, experimentally, past the horses, his eyes keen for any signs of further disturbance, then, satisfied, he slid it into top gear and shortly afterwards dropped his charges, protesting, into the hands of the hospital Casualty Department.

'I'm responsible for them,' was all he replied when told by the nurse in charge that he need not wait, and he seated himself on one of the hard waiting room chairs as if he was prepared to sit there all day if necessary. Roma wriggled uneasily on the chair next to his, her mind teeming with questions to which she could find no satisfactory answers.

Was Willy's wrist broken? And if it was, what effect would it have on his riding? Had Silver Cloud been injured when she reared and went over backwards? Most of all, what did Earl intend to do about the young firework thrower? That it was a deliberate act of vengeance because the trainer took the apples from him, that day in the Lodge garden, she did not doubt. All too clearly she heard again the young, defiant voice shout, 'I'll get me own back, I will!' He had got his own back with a vengeance, she thought worriedly, and one look at Earl's stern countenance told her that the boy would not escape the reckoning this time so easily as he had done the last.

'It was only a childish prank,' she ventured at last, unable to keep silent any longer. 'Jimmy's too young to realise. . . .' She ground to a halt as she met Earl's steely glance.

'Jimmy's shortly due to grow up, and be *made* to realise,' he retorted sternly. 'Any one of those riders today could have been seriously injured as a result of him throwing that firework at the horses.'

'It was—horrible,' she shuddered, shaking still at the memory of the stampeding thoroughbreds.

'Perhaps after witnessing the results of just one firework,' Earl added with biting emphasis, 'you'll realise why it is I won't allow bonfires anywhere near the stables. I've got thousands of pounds' worth of bloodstock entrusted to my care, all of them in prime racing condition. I hate to think what effect today's episode will have on their form,' he frowned. 'The black's due to race at Cheltenham tomorrow.'

'Oh, the horses! It's always the horses!' She rounded on him, her voice shrill, the aftermath of fright and shock exploding in a petulant outburst. 'Just for a second I thought your first concern might be for the stable lads, but of course it's the horses. I might have known,' she cried scornfully.

'Riding is part of the stable lads' work. They know the risks they take, when they apply for their jobs.'

'They're too young to be in charge of horses of that calibre,' Roma insisted stubbornly. 'You said yourself that thoroughbreds are highly strung and nervous, and you admitted they can be dangerous.'

'For heaven's sake, woman,' Earl gritted tensely, 'how old do you think an apprentice jockey has to be? Forty?'

Roma did not care if it was four hundred. She felt as unnerved as the horses by the incident, and the chaotic state of her feelings expended itself in anger against Earl.

'Bob doesn't seem capable of remaining on Silver

Cloud's back,' she retorted waspishly. It was a criminal libel, but she ruthlessly stifled any feelings of guilt and rushed on recklessly. 'If Mick had been riding her, he would have stuck on her. He wouldn't have let her throw herself over like that. She might easily have injured herself.'

'Even Mick wouldn't have been prepared for a firework to be hurled at him,' Earl snapped back. 'No one could possibly have foreseen that such a thing would happen.'

'An older man would have been able to cope with an emergency, even one as bad as that.'

'Professional jockeys don't spend their time exercising stable strings,' Earl's voice was tight, clipped, dismissing her opinions as worthless, contemptuous of her lack of knowledge of his world. 'Bob's more than capable of coping with the grey. But if you don't think so,' he growled ominously, 'if you're not satisfied with the attention Silver Cloud's getting at Burdon Court, you're at liberty to take your horse elsewhere.'

'That's just the trouble—I haven't got that liberty, not even with my own horse,' she retorted bitterly, her resentment at Earl's right to control the grey boiling over in an angry surge of words. 'If I had, I'd take her away immediately,' she declared forthrightly, 'but under the terms of the will. . . .'

'Just as soon as the Vintners' Stakes are run, I'll waive the terms of the will, and you can take the grey where you please,' Earl answered her grimly.

'I won't wait for the Vintners' Stakes, whatever they might be,' she flung at him defiantly.

'I won't release the grey until after the Stakes,' Earl began, and Roma's temper snapped.

'Silver Cloud belongs to me, not to you. She's my inheritance,' she cried furiously.

'And entrusted to me to train,' he thrust back curtly. 'I won't have all the work I've put into her undone by an owner who doesn't know the first thing about racing. I won't have the filly's chances spoiled by a raw amateur who only wants the animal to satisfy her own ego,' he told her bitingly. 'A girl who's little else but a silly filly herself.'

'How dare you!' The man was absolutely insufferable! she fumed.

'I dare because I think Silver Cloud's a great horse with a fine future. She deserves the chance to realise her potential, and I intend to see that she gets it.' He would do anything for the horse. If only he felt the same way about herself! Roma's heart contracted with an almost unbearable agony, because it was the horse he was concerned for, and not herself, and out of the agony she lashed out at him with angry words, striking out at him because he was the cause of it.

'I suppose this pettifogging little race you seem to set such store by is due to be run in about twelve months' time?' she suggested with bitter sarcasm, and resolutely kept her eyes averted so that he might not see their sudden mistiness.

'It's anything but a little event,' Earl retorted tersely. 'It's known throughout the sport as a testing race, and it's due to be run in a fortnight's time. Only the cream of the season's two-year-olds are ever considered good enough to enter, even the more experienced horses have to be in top form to compete. It's the race for which I've trained Silver Cloud specially. The results of the Vintners' Stakes can make or break the start of her racing career. On her present form, the filly's got every chance of winning, and if she does it'll enhance her chances for the rest of the season, and double her value.'

'I suppose you've entered Arabian Minty as well?' she asked, and her tone was loaded with meaning.

'Minty's entered, yes,' he replied shortly. 'The gelding's got a good chance.'

'In that case, Silver Cloud hasn't,' Roma retorted bitterly. 'You'll see to that. You'll enter the grey as a pacer again, the same as you did at Auteuil,' she accused him wildly.

She quailed before the steel in his look. He turned right round in his chair and glowered at her, and the angry, burning glare frightened her more than the firework had frightened the horses. She caught her breath in an agonised gasp.

'Earl, I. . . .' His look stopped the words in her throat, his rock-hard face took them away and reduced her to quivering silence, and he spoke into that silence in a clipped, tight voice, that sounded like the knell of doom in her startled ears.

'Silver Cloud is entered to run—to win,' he emphasised, 'not to pace.' His words hit her, each like a single, individual hammer blow, but she did not doubt that they were true. 'I won't have the filly upset by a change of trainer before the race, any change in routine puts a horse off its stroke, and the grey's in top form now, and deserves the chance to show her paces. After the race is over, you can take your horse to whichever training establishment is willing to accept her,' he told Roma with harsh finality, and turned his back on her abruptly as the nurse in charge of the Casualty Department appeared, ushering two subdued-looking stable lads in their direction, and announced with professional brightness,

'No bones broken. This one's got a badly sprained wrist, and this one's scratched to ribbons, but they'll survive.'

'Whichever training establishment is willing to accept her.'

Roma hardly heard the nurse. She stared with unseeing eyes at Earl's back. His straight, uncompromising back, like a solid wall turned against her, shutting her out, and the implications of what he said sank into her consciousness with a cold foreboding. It had not occurred to her that a trainer might not be willing to accept her horse into his stables. To appease her pride she had toyed often enough with the idea of removing Silver Cloud from Burdon Court, relishing the thought, hugging it to her as a balm to her bruised feelings. It would be the perfect stroke, the final coup de grâce that would assert her own independence, and humble Earl's arrogant pride. But always, in her imagination, it had been herself who was to be the instigator of such a move, not Earl.

Now—she swallowed, and her throat felt suddenly dry. Now, out of the blue, it was the other way round. *Earl* was telling *her* to take the grey elsewhere. The set of his jaw told her that he meant it, and would be unlikely to change his mind no matter what she said. It did not help that she had provoked the confrontation, and must now face up to, not just an imaginary threat, but the harsh reality that in two weeks' time she would have to find a new trainer for Silver Cloud. She did not know how to even start looking for another trainer, she thought desperately. She did not *know* any other racehorse trainer, except Earl.

Her mind raced in dizzy circles until she began to feel as if she might shortly need the attention of the Casualty Department staff herself, as the unpalatable truth sank in that, when she removed the grey from Earl's stables, pride would forbid that she should herself remain under the trainer's roof. Which meant that, unless the Lodge could be made ready for her to move into within the next two weeks, and the builder's estimate told her that was clearly impossible, at the end of that time she, as well as Silver Cloud, would be homeless.

CHAPTER TEN

'It's a good job Mr Paget was with you. It would have been a frightening thing if you'd been stranded on your own, in that fog. You couldn't see a hand in front of you here, last night,' Mrs Murray tut-tutted at the vagaries of the weather, and Roma felt a surge of irritation at her well-meant sympathy.

She ought to have felt thankful. She had been more concerned than she cared to admit at what might be Mrs Murray's reaction to the news that she had spent the night stranded at the roadside, with Earl. She had taken a liking to the Burdon Court housekeeper, and had no wish to fall from grace in her esteem. Perversely, her relief turned to irritation.

'It was frightening enough, as it was.' It was not the fog that had terrified her, but the overwhelming force of her own feelings, when Earl kissed her. The knowledge that Earl had moved in and taken over, and she would never completely belong to herself, ever again.

'Eh well, there's no harm done.' Only to her heart, and that did not seem to matter to anybody but herself, Roma thought bleakly. 'You were safe enough with Mr Paget. The only telephone call we had was from that Mr Blantyre, and I told him you were both stranded in the fog.'

What would Horace Blantyre make of that? Roma wondered wryly. She doubted very much if he would take the same charitable view of her safety as Mrs Murray. And anyway, why should she be so safe with Earl? she asked herself crossly. He was a man, wasn't he? Subject to the same temptations as other men? The housekeeper acted as if he could do no wrong, and Steve was just as bad. The head lad greeted their return into the stable yard with a cheerful,

'We guessed you'd had to pull in somewhere along the route. I'll bet you were thankful you weren't driving on your own, Miss Roma? At least we knew you'd be all right with the Guv'nor.'

To which Roma would have liked to reply, but dared not.

'I wish I had been on my own. I'd rather be frightened of the fog than frightened of myself.' She could leave the fog behind, as soon as it dispersed with the daylight it was gone, and forgotten. But she could not forget herself. She could not leave her own aroused feelings behind. They travelled along with her, tormenting her. Taunting her with the knowledge that life could never be the same again, the life she knew was gone, and the one she longed for would never come, and she must somehow come to terms with an existence in between the two that held neither interest nor attraction, because it did not also hold Earl.

'We could have done without the reception we received in Down Burdon.' Briefly Earl outlined to Steve what had happened.

'I know, Dave's wife rang us up in a panic,' Steve nodded, 'but she said you were there, so I didn't come out myself, I sent Dave off with four of the lads and waited on here for you to come in.'

'Evidently he thinks if Earl's present, no one else is necessary,' Roma told herself waspishly, but before she could say anything, Steve went on,

'Are these the only two casualties?' He eyed the liberally bandaged lads who eased themselves down out of the Range Rover with painful caution.

'Yes, they can be excused from duties for the next two days. No longer,' Earl told him crisply. 'I'll help out at stables, and take their turn on watch tonight.'

'Does that mean we can go to the bonfire, Guv'nor?' Although Earl spoke quietly enough to Steve, the two boys must have had pricked ears, and they both perked up visibly at the unexpected bonus of free time.

'Well, I'll be . . .!' Steve exclaimed.

'Let them go, if they're fit enough.' Earl's lips twitched, then straightened again as he turned to the two lads. 'Mind and be back again by ten o'clock, the same as the other lads. Not a minute later,' he warned the pair sternly.

He could have relaxed stable discipline just for once, Roma thought disgustedly. The boys had been injured riding his horses. From their cheerful grins it seemed that the prospect of the bonfire had better curative properties than the hospital treatment, and she envied them their quick resilience of spirit. Earl had not said anything about her going to the bonfire. She checked her thoughts sharply.

'Don't be so spineless!' She heaped scorn on her own lack of spirit. 'You don't have to ask Earl's permission. You're a free agent, you can go where you please, and do whatever you please, without going cap in hand to him.' She returned to the house and shut the door behind

her with a decided bang. 'I'll go to the bonfire with the
stable lads,' she declared out loud, and tried to tell herself she was looking forward to the evening's celebra-
tions.

But when she got there, she discovered she did not want
to remain. 'Why did I come?' She regretted her hasty
stand for independence as she cringed away from the
sparks and the whirling lights. She had always been nervous of fireworks, and on top of the events of the last
twenty-four hours they proved too much for her new
found resolution. 'I've got a bit of a headache,' she but-
tonholed Willy, who seemed to be thoroughly enjoying
himself in spite of his bandaged wrist. 'I think I'll walk
back home.' She refused his gallant offer to leave the
festivities and walk with her. 'A quiet stroll might take
it away before bedtime.'

It seemed extra dark in the lanes after the noise and
the lights of the bonfire. The river murmured sleepily to
itself between its high banks on the one side of the lane,
and Roma slowed her steps, soothed by the gentle sound
of the water. She crossed the lane to walk beside it, unconsciously seeking its company.

'Thank goodness it's not foggy,' she muttered thankfully. The night was clear and still, with stars showing
between the gaps in the overhanging trees. She turned up
the collar of her jacket and thrust her hands into her
pockets, searching for the pair of woollen gloves she had
thrust there when the bonfire made their cosy comfort
unnecessary.

'I must have dropped them,' she frowned. 'Oh well,
they were old ones, anyway. They're probably gracing
the Guy by now.' She shrugged and carried on walking,
unwilling to retrace her steps to retrieve them, reluctant
to return too soon to Burdon Court, and Earl. She
wondered idly what he was doing, and stifled a small pang
of guilt that she had not mentioned where she intended to
go to, after dinner. It was not the behaviour of a con-
siderate guest, to disappear without trace.

'I don't have to report my every movement to Earl.

I'm not one of his employees,' she excused herself stoutly, and thrust away the desolate thought that he probably had not noticed her absence anyway. He would be too intent on patrolling his stables, attending to the needs of his horses. Always, the horses. . . .

'What on earth are you doing, wandering the lanes on your own after dark?'

'Oh, my goodness!' Roma jumped violently as what she had taken to be part of a tree trunk, suddenly detached itself from the roadside and demanded an explanation of her presence in an angry voice. Earl's voice.

'Do you have to spring out at people from dark hedgerows?' she cried furiously. 'You gave me the fright of my life.' Her heart hammered suffocatingly fast, and she tried to tell herself it was only fright that was to blame, and knew that it was not. If it had been Steve, or Mick, or one of the stable lads, the violent palpitation would have quietened as quickly as it started. But it was not a member of the stable staff. It was Earl himself, and the grip of his fingers as he caught her by the arm accelerated her heartbeat to racing speed, until she felt sure he must feel the vibration of its wild beating, as she had only that morning, on this selfsame lane, felt the vibration of racing hooves beat into her through its hard surface.

'It's not safe for you to walk the lanes after dark.'

'Don't be silly,' she laughed him to scorn, interrupting him. She felt quite proud of her laugh. It was breathless, and shaky, and it took all her willpower to produce, but somehow she managed it, and the darkness hid the white-faced effort it cost her. 'I'm not a child, to be frightened of shadows,' she exclaimed.

'I'm talking of something more substantial than shadows. Like traffic, for instance.' Earl hauled her back on to the verge with him as a pair of car lights cut blindingly across them from round the corner. 'You're wearing dark clothing,' he said accusingly.

'That's not a crime,' Roma flared rebelliously.

'It makes you inconspicuous to the driver of a car,' he went on relentlessly, as if she had not spoken, 'and to make matters worse, you were walking on the wrong side of the lane.'

Matters could hardly be much worse than they were, she told herself wretchedly. She had come to the bonfire to escape Earl. She had come away from the bonfire to escape the noise and the people, to be by herself, and to use the darkness and the solitude to try and sort her chaotic emotions into some sort of order that would enable her to regain at least an outward semblance of poise before she had to face Earl again. And now he was here, in the lane with her, and what was worse he was holding her, with both arms ringing her to prevent her from stepping into the path of the oncoming car, which surely could not have done so much damage as the feel of his arms around her, the feel of his closeness against her, was doing now?

'Your own clothing isn't exactly fluorescent,' she reminded him bitingly, stung by his accusation, and galled by the knowledge that partly, at least, it was justified. She resolutely ignored the fact that Earl's tweed jacket swung wide open, revealing an expanse of white, polo-necked sweater, and he was walking on the side of the lane so that he faced the oncoming traffic, to which the white sweater would show up as clearly as a beacon in the headlights. She hurried on, before he had time to expose the weakness of her counter-thrust. 'What are you doing here, anyway? You said you were going to be on watch at the stables tonight. You promised to take Sean's and Willy's turn. Don't tell me you decided to come and enjoy the bonfire, after all?' she asked him sarcastically.

'On the contrary,' he replied evenly, 'I came to meet you.'

'To meet me?' She stared up at him in the darkness, disbelievingly. 'How did you know . . .?'

'Because Dave's wife rang the Court to say she'd found your gloves, and that she'd give them to one of the stable lads to bring back for you. One of the lads should have walked you home,' Earl added, in a tone that boded ill for the ones responsible for the omission.

'They did offer to, and I wouldn't let them,' Roma

defended them, and added cuttingly, 'I wanted to be on my own.' That should dispose of his arrogant assumption that his own company was welcome to her, she told herself fiercely.

'You can be on your own just as much as you want to, the moment you're back indoors at the Court,' he retorted in a hard voice. 'I've got work to do.'

'I didn't ask you to neglect it, to come and meet me,' she reminded him tartly. 'So far as I'm concerned, you needn't have bothered. After the Vintners' Stakes, you won't have to bother about me, or my horse, any more.' Her chin came up in a defiant gesture that completely lost its impact because of the darkness.

'As soon as you've found another trainer, let me know,' Earl gritted, and swung her off the lane and through the Lodge gates at a speed that made her trot to keep up with him.

'I don't anticipate any trouble finding one who'll take Silver Cloud,' she thrust back with a confidence she did not feel. 'I don't doubt there'll be plenty of trainers at the racecourse tomorrow. I'll fix up something with one of them. Maybe I'll ask Horace Blantyre if he can recommend one,' she taunted.

'Blantyre? Hah!' Earl snorted explosively. 'The man's got more knowledge of a bar counter than he has of racing. Stay away from him,' he ordered her brusquely. 'He's not your type.'

'How do you know who's my type?' she flung back at him. 'If I want to ask Horace Blantyre, I'll do so. At least he shows more concern for his horse than you do for your stable lads.' It was grossly unjust, but it was the only weapon she had, and he thrust aside its barb with contemptuous indifference.

'Apprentice jockeys don't expect to be fussed over, they accept the risks inherent in their jobs. And as for showing concern,' his voice lashed her, harsh and condemnatory through the darkness, 'you don't exactly excel in that particular sphere yourself.'

'I did everything I possibly could for Willy and Sean,'

she defended herself vigorously. 'Willy was the only one who was really much hurt. Sean got badly scratched, I know. . . .'

'And so did I,' he reminded her shortly, 'so if you're talking about concern. . . .' At the entrance to the Burdon Court gardens he suddenly halted, and before she was aware of what he was about to do, he pulled her round to face him. 'By the time I'd hauled Sean out of that bramble patch,' he reminded her grimly, 'my face and hands looked as if I'd been in a fight with a wildcat.'

The young moon confirmed what he said, touching lightly on a livid scratch that scored his lean face from forehead to jaw. Her startled eyes traced its length as he bent his head low over her upturned face.

'So, if you've got any concern to spare. . . .' he grated.

'No!' She dared not let him kiss her again. The memory of what happened to her when he kissed her the night before, washed over her in a terrifying humiliating flood. She had only just managed to regain some semblance of calm, and now. . . . Once his lips touched her own, it would all come back, the longing, the heartbreak. To Earl it was a moment's amusement, but to her it was torture. Each time he kissed her, her heart died a little within her, because his kisses meant nothing—to him. But each one intensified her pain until it was more than she could bear. She dared not let it happen again.

'No!'

She twisted violently in his arms, beating her head against his chest, crushing her face close into the warm woollen softness of his sweater, her hair a dark silhouette against its stark whiteness, so that his lips should not reach her own.

'You showed a commendable concern for the stable lads,' he snarled, and his lips descended on the top of her head, pressing down on her hair.

It felt as if a spear of lightning burned right through her, from head to toe. She went rigid in his arms, and then, suddenly, all the accumulated fear and pain and anguish exploded like an enormous firework inside her.

Careless of anything except the need to get away, she fought him with all her strength. If he thought the bramble patch resembled a wildcat, she thought hysterically, he must now believe he held one in his arms! She hammered against him with her clenched fists, beating him to try to force him to release her. Terror lent her the strength of the possessed.

'Let me go . . .!'

She squirmed and twisted and struggled, her breath hissing in harsh, panting gasps through her set teeth, while tears of desperation coursed across her cheeks like rain.

'Let me go,' she sobbed, and without warning went limp in his arms. Her ears throbbed with the force of her passion, and the world spun dizzily round her.

'Roma?' His arms slackened their grip slightly, and his voice reached her as if through a dark mist, forceful, and sharp. Concerned? More likely shouting at her, she guessed angrily. The anger saved her. The dizziness fled before it, leaving her senses clear again, raw with pain, and the need to escape. With a final, convulsive movement she took advantage of his slackened grip and wrenched herself free.

'Leave me alone. Just leave me alone!' she sobbed wildly, and stumbled blindly away from him, across the moonlit garden, towards where her flooded eyes could just discern the dark outline of the house, rising solid against the stars, offering shelter, sanctuary, and blessed privacy, where her tears could flow unchecked, and where nothing but the softness of her pillow listened to the strangled sobs that were wrenched from her aching throat by stark despair.

Skilfully applied make-up covered the worst of the ravages the next morning, and she hurried through a token breakfast, her mind made up.

'I'll find out the names of one of two trainers, and then make some definite arrangements for Silver Cloud's accommodation,' she determined. Having something positive to do helped a little, she discovered, and closed her mind to the fact that she must very soon make similar arrangements for herself.

'I'll think of that when I feel a bit stronger,' she prevaricated. Telltale dark smudges marked her eyes, betraying the devastation left by the storm that destroyed her sleep the night before, and left her to face another dawn with spirits as dark as the night itself.

'I must get Silver Cloud's future settled.' Her forehead puckered in a worried frown, and she forced herself into her anorak, and along the path that led to the stable yard. For the first time, she did not care how she looked to Earl. The pale blue woolly over her white shirt blouse would have to do—it no longer mattered, she told herself listlessly. She eyed her perfume, and for a brief, rejuvenated second she felt tempted to use the phial that Flip Dean had given her, but even as she reached out her hand to take it up, caution overruled defiance.

'I don't think I can face another row with Earl today,' she muttered, and reluctantly reached for the gift the trainer had given to her instead. It was the only other perfume she had with her, at Burdon Court, and although she did not want to use it, she needed something to boost her confidence.

'We'll be ready to go in about ten minutes, Miss Roma,' Steve greeted her from beside the Range Rover as she entered the stable yard. 'It should be a good day, today, the black seems no worse for his fright yesterday.'

Which was more than could be said for herself, Roma thought ruefully, but aloud she asked,

'Where's . . .?' She could not see Mick anywhere, and surely he must be coming with them? Earl had said he would be riding the black colt.

'Where's the Guv'nor?' Steve misunderstood her. 'He's just checking on the bay colt that bolted yesterday, he won't be long. By the time Dave caught up with it, the horse had managed to strain a tendon.'

'Is that bad?' There did not seem to be any point in her learning about horses any longer, she thought drearily, but at least it made some sort of conversation, and helped to keep at bay the silence which allowed her own, unwanted, thoughts to take over, and that she must prevent at any cost, because her thoughts were self inflicted pain.

'Nothing that hot fomentations won't cure,' Steve answered confidently. 'Here's the Guv'nor, now,' he went on as Earl appeared silhouetted in the lamplight of the stable door. 'I'll go and get my jacket from the tack room, then we can be on our way.'

'I'll fetch it for you,' Roma offered breathlessly. She did not want to be left alone with Earl, not even for the few minutes that it would take Steve to go to the tack room and back, and she hastened away before the head lad could refuse her. He called after her,

'Don't switch on the light in the tack room, Miss Roma. There's something wrong with the switch. It seems to be shorting, or something. . . .'

'I won't,' Roma called back over her shoulder, without stopping. There was sufficient light for her to be able to see, if she left the tack room door open. The young day was growing stronger by the minute, and she found the jacket without trouble. It was draped across a chair seat, and the black kitten was curled up comfortably on top.

'Perhaps you'll bring us luck.' She gave the little animal a quick cuddle, and was rewarded by a sleepy purr, and setting it back comfortably on the chair cushion she hurried out with the jacket, and handed it over to Steve.

'Let's hope we have better luck with the weather, today,' Mick greeted her cheerfully as he joined them, making the party complete.

'We'll make sure and start back early, this time,' said Earl, and slanted a glance at Roma that brought an angry flush to her cheeks.

'You were driving the last time, so it was up to you when we started back,' she retorted unfairly, thrusting the blame back on to his shoulders. They were square, and straight, and supported the strong brown column of his neck in a way that did odd things to her heart, and made her wish she had not taken the seat directly behind him in the vehicle, where she could not help but look at his shoulders. She had sat there deliberately, so that Earl should not be able to see her if he chanced to look round, but now, each time she looked up, she met his eyes in the rear view mirror, and she wished she had sat behind Mick instead. She looked away hurriedly, and from then onwards kept her head rigidly averted, staring with unseeing eyes through the window beside her until it seemed as if her neck must be locked for life in the one direction.

'Thank goodness Cheltenham isn't so far away as Newmarket.'

Just when it began to seem as if the journey would never end, a sudden build-up of traffic heralded the approach to the town, and a frustrating start/stop road crawl on to the racecourse itself, which surely, Roma thought as she slid out of the vehicle on Mick's side of the car, ignoring the door which Earl held open for her on the other side, must be blessed with the loveliest setting of any racecourse in the country. She gladly assented to Mick's invitation,

'Come with us, Roma. We're going to walk the course before the racing starts.'

'Haven't you raced here before?' she asked him, surprised.

'Dozens of times,' the little Irishman laughed, 'but it always pays to take another look from off your own feet. You're going too fast when you're in the saddle to notice very much except the horse that's breathing down your neck, trying to overtake you,' he said cheerfully.

It was the same meticulous attention to detail that Earl practised himself, and insisted on from all his staff. The unremitting thoroughness that put all the horses he trained into the winning classes, and, thought Roma uneasily, gave him a waiting list of owners from whom he could choose the mounts he wished to work with. From whom he could quite easily choose one to fill the place now occupied by Silver Cloud.

'A penny for your thoughts?' Mick teased her on her silence, but she smiled and shook her head, refusing to be drawn. This was a problem she could not share with the friendly little jockey. Earl's stable staff were loyal, in spite of his strictness he seemed able to inspire an allegiance from his employees that would regard talk of another trainer as little short of traitorous, she realised unhappily. She would have to turn to Horace Blantyre for advice, there was no one else she knew of who could help her in her present dilemma.

In anticipation, it had seemed so easy, to casually mention that she was looking for another trainer. In her imagination she received an equally casual answer, giving her just the information she needed, and she had already planned her next move from there. A telephone call, a personal inspection of the new trainer's stables, and that would be that. Silver Cloud would have accommodation, and she would be free to find a home for herself until the Lodge was ready. It would then only need Silver Cloud to win an important race under the new trainer to vindicate her decision to move the grey, and show Earl that she was capable of running her own life without his interference, she told herself vengefully.

'I hope you've put something on the black's chances, Miss Forrester?'

Horace Blantyre was even more repulsive than she remembered him. She had no love for the black colt, but she preferred the horse to its owner, she decided, regarding his waddling approach with distaste. At least, the horse had breeding.

'I don't bet.' She tried to instil some warmth into her voice, and failed signally. Her tone dripped ice. She could not help it. It condemned the suggestion, and the man for making it. With a kind of detached interest she saw an answering, angry gleam appear in the small, fat-ringed eyes, and knew without caring that she had made an enemy.

'I can't ask his advice about another trainer now.'

Relief and dismay fought for supremacy as the realisation hit her that she had irretrievably burned her boats, and that she knew of no one else to whom she could turn to for advice. She should have known better than to believe she could ask Horace Blantyre to help her in the first

place. What had Earl said? 'He's not your type.' She
wished the man would leave them, and knew that it was
out of the question, since it was inevitable that owner and
trainer should come together in their mutual interest in
the race. She turned away to watch the now familiar
bustle on the course with a curious feeling of detachment.
The line-up. The eager burst of speed at the start. The
battle for supremacy that weeded out the runners in mid-
field, and then one lone runner, pulling out ahead of the
rest of the field. But when Mick on the black passed the
finishing post at least two lengths ahead of their rivals,
she felt no jubilation, nothing, except a heavy thankfulness that the race was over, and they would soon be
able to take their leave of Horace Blantyre, and go back
home. Back to Burdon Court, she amended. It would
soon be 'home' to her no longer.

Her hope was shortlived.

'You've got to come and help me to celebrate my win.'
Horace Blantyre slapped Earl on the back with jubilant
familiarity. He had to reach up to do it, Roma noticed
with an inward grin, which became more and more forced
as some time later her fellow racehorse owner, brandishing
his newly won trophy, pressed drinks on all and sundry,
and joined in each round himself with an enthusiasm
which made Roma hope fervently he did not intend to
attempt to drive himself home.

'I really don't want. . . .' she began, desperately trying
to fend off an unwanted refill of her scarcely touched glass,
and sent Earl a look that pleaded with him to extricate
her from a situation that was rapidly growing untenable.
She did not like wine, she had never liked wine, and she
did not want to drink it now, particularly with Horace
Blantyre, whom she liked even less.

'Pour it into that aspidistra thing, just behind you,' Earl
murmured in her ear. 'I've already sent mine in that
direction. . . .'

It was all Roma could do not to giggle out loud.
Laughter lit her eyes and tilted up the corners of her lips
in an irrepressible arc.

'My horse showed the way home to the rest of the field,' Horace Blantyre boasted loudly. 'He showed them all the way home.' He looked up, and met Roma's eyes.

'He thinks I'm laughing at him.'

She was not. She did not find his half-inebriated appearance in the least funny. The black's owner patently felt the same about her expression. His own changed as their glances locked, and Roma caught a dismayed breath. Her refusal to place a bet on the black colt had offended him badly, and now her smile was the last straw. His angry glare told her that he took her refusal as a personal affront.

'Maybe you should have borrowed the black, to show you the way home from the yearling sales,' he sneered unpleasantly. 'Or perhaps you preferred things as they were, eh? Fog makes a convenient excuse,' he suggested with a spiteful leer.

'How dare you!' Roma gasped at his effrontery, and put down her glass on a nearby table with an angry click.

'You needn't act all high and mighty with me, miss,' his eyes glittered vengefully in his puffy face. 'I know you spent the night out with your posh trainer, after you left the yearling sales. Stranded in the fog, his housekeeper told me when I rang to ask about the colt. A fine excuse, I must say,' he jeered with drunken recklessness. 'I saw the scratch you put across Paget's face.' He thrust his own close to Roma's, and she backed away in disgust as a wave of whisky-laden breath hit her like an atomic cloud. 'Didn't you like your trainer's attentions, then, my little filly? Is that why you scratched his face for him? For all your fine airs and graces,' he spat vindictively, 'you're nothing but. . . .'

'That's enough!'

Earl's voice cut like a whiplash through the suddenly silent room. Roma's face went scarlet, and then deathly white. The silence was absolute. Even the barman stopped clinking his glasses. It seemed, she thought bewilderedly, as if everyone stopped breathing. She felt suffocated, herself. She wanted to run away. She wanted to remain, and shout to the room at large that the odious man's even more odious suggestion, was not true. And then, quite suddenly, she wanted to cry.

'Earl?' Her voice was a thin whisper, begging his help for the second time that afternoon. She felt as if she was standing on her own, on the top of a high hill, with no-where to hide, and everyone was staring at her. There seemed to be literally hundreds of eyes in the room, all looking at her. All wondering. . . .

'Earl?'

Why did he not speak? she asked herself passionately. Why did he not shout at Horace Blantyre, deny his in-famous suggestion, make him apologise?

'Mick, take Roma outside, and wait for me in the car.'

She stared at Earl, stunned. He was not making the slightest attempt to deny the jibes, to clear her good name. Instead of turning on Horace Blantyre and slaying him with angry words, he was sending her away, dismissing her, she thought disbelievingly, as if it was she who was at fault. Well, if Earl could not stand up for her, she would have to stand up for herself, she thought furiously.

'Come with me, Roma love. Come away,' Mick coaxed gently, and his small brown hand grasped her fingers that felt suddenly icy cold. Just as suddenly, the fire of battle left her, and she felt drained, and empty of feeling, except that the desire to cry returned, stronger than ever, refusing to be denied, and she could not—must not—cry in front of Horace Blantyre. Or in front of Earl. She must get away, before the tears forced themselves out of her smart-ing eyes, and proved the final humiliation. Blindly she grasped Mick's hand and stumbled after him through the door, clinging to him like a child needing to be led.

'There now,' he crooned, and helped her to fasten the seat belt, settling her into the passenger seat of the Range Rover; his own seat, the one next to Earl, but she felt too sick and shaken by the scene she had just left to be able to summon up the energy to protest. 'We'll be on our way home in a jiffy and less,' the little jockey comforted. 'Here come the Guv'nor and Steve now. That didn't take long,' he added with satisfaction, and Roma wondered what 'that' had been, but before she could put her thoughts into words Earl climbed into the driving seat next to her, looked down at her with a keen, searching glance, and she tried to meet it, and found she could not. She tried to cry out to him, accuse him of his treachery, denounce him for not raising his voice in her defence, but drowning in the dark peat pool depths of his enigmatic stare the words died in her throat, unsaid, and he looked away again, releasing her, and nodded to Mick, giving the jockey a soundless answer to a wordless question, and she felt too numb to guess what either might be.

The silence inside the Range Rover was as total as that in the room she had just left, pregnant with questions she dared not ask, and answers she did not want to hear. The engine purred smoothly, seeming to deepen the silence rather than to break it, and she lay back in the luxurious upholstery and closed her eyes, but her weary lids refused to hold back the slow tears that found their way under the sooty fringe of lashes, and trickled down her cheeks. She felt nauseated at the mere thought of Horace Blantyre's insinuations. Far from obtaining the help she had hoped for from him, he had done his best to defame her. And now, on top of being faced with losing her own accommodation and that of her horse, she had lost her character as well, she thought bitterly. And it was all Earl's fault.

She must have slept. The clanging of an alarm bell roused her. It was too loud, and too insistent, to be her bedside alarm clock. It seemed to be following her, coming nearer . . . nearer. . . .

'Oh, my goodness!' It was right beside her, clangingly, terrifyingly loud, broadcasting a warning of she knew not what. Both her hands rose to press against her ears to shut out the sound, to shut out the fear. The Range Rover swerved and stopped, and her eyes flew wide open, startled into full wakefulness as Earl pulled the vehicle hurriedly into a field gateway to allow the bright scarlet fire engine to pass on its urgent way.

'We're nearly home,' she realised, recognising the familiar church, the row of cottages, and the fork in the lane ahead.

'Surely they're not having trouble with the village bonfire.' Steve watched the fleeing fire engine with alert eyes. 'It should have been burned out by now.'

'He isn't going to the bonfire.' Mick leaned forward tensely as the scarlet vehicle swung along the left-hand fork which led away from the village. 'Get a move on, Guv'nor,' he urged Earl in a taut voice. 'Follow behind the engine.'

'Where's it going?' Roma began, and her spine tingled as back came the terse reply,

'There's only one place it can be going, along that lane. It's heading for Burdon Court stables!'

CHAPTER ELEVEN

IT was like a scene from a nightmare. Smoke poured from the tack room roof, and tongues of orange flame licked hungrily round the window frames. Even as Roma watched, the glass panes exploded with the heat, and sent a shower of lethal splinters scattering across the cobbles of the stable yard. Earl pulled the Range Rover to a halt behind the fire engine, and in a trice the three men jumped to the ground.

'Help to clear the stables nearest the tack room,' Earl called to Mick and Steve, and then swung back to Roma as he was about to run after them. 'Stay here,' he commanded her, 'you'll be safe in the car.'

Acrid smoke swirled through the open window, and made her cough. The firemen ran out hosepipes with disciplined efficiency. The bell had stopped clanging, but the noises that assailed her frightened ears were even worse than the bell, she decided shudderingly. High-pitched screams from the horses rent the air as the smell of smoke penetrated their stalls, unleashing the worst fear known to every living creature, the inborn dread of fire. A series of crashes, and dreadful splintering sounds, echoed from the stable nearest to the tack room, the one worst afflicted by the smoke. It was the stall that housed the bay colt which had bolted the previous day. In a frenzy of fear, it was trying to kick its way free from its stall. Roma saw Steve run through the smoke towards it, and heard Earl shout,

'The next one—go to the next one! I'll deal with the bay.' He gestured the head lad away from the door and headed towards the stall himself, dragging off his jacket as he ran.

'Earl, be careful! Be careful. . . .'

She froze with fear as he swung open the stable door and disappeared inside. Minutes passed, agonising minutes, each one of them a lifetime long. The kicking went on, dreadful banging sounds as iron-shod hooves struck wood. And then the sounds stopped, and a wave of faintness made the stable yard go dark in front of Roma's eyes. Horseshoes would make no banging sound against the softness of a human body. . . .

'Earl. Earl, darling. . . .'

A sob tore through her, a strangled, anguished sound that she did not recognise as coming from her own throat. Her eyes blurred, turning the scene in the stable yard into a macabre dance. Moving figures wavered dizzily into her line of vision, barely recognisable through the tears and the smoke. Something bulky moved jerkily in the open stable door through which Earl had disappeared. It looked weird and distorted, like a huge, disjointed horse, and it was wearing Earl's jacket.

'I must be going mad!'

'Hold on, Guv'nor, I'll give you a hand to lead him.'

The jockey's shout cleared the darkness from Roma's mind, and with desperate fingers she rubbed the tears from her eyes, and saw through the open car window. . . .

'Earl!' He was safe. The horse hadn't kicked him. 'Earl. . . .'

The weird creature in the stable door was, indeed, a

horse. It was the bay that had reduced its stall to match-wood. And it *was* wearing Earl's jacket. She caught her breath in an hysterical half laugh, half sob of relief. The trainer had draped his tweed over the colt's head, covering its eyes and nose so that it could not see the flames, and for the moment anyway, could not smell the smoke. It shied nervously at the unseen bustle of strange sounds, but patiently Earl talked to it, coaxing it through the stable door, choking and coughing himself from the smoke, but ignoring his own distress until he had the animal into the comparatively clear air of the stable yard.

'I'll take this side of him.' Mick ran to grasp one side of the bay's halter while Earl held the other, and their combined weight kept the colt down on all fours so that it could no longer rear.

'The others are all out. They came quieter than this one.'

'Take them into the indoor training area, rug them up, and walk them round until they've calmed down,' Earl instructed him. 'I'll join you when I've attended to things here.' He indicated the firemen who, the flames extinguished, were starting to uncouple their hoses, while the leader of the team approached him.

'Everything's damped down now, Mr Paget,' he said briskly. 'Two of my men are making a final check to see that everything's safe to be left. And, of course, the electricity's been switched off,' he warned. 'You won't be able to use the stable circuit until tomorrow, I'm afraid. You'll have to get an electrician in to see to it.'

'The electricity?' Earl frowned. 'Why . . .?'

'It seems as if you had a faulty switch in the tack room, sir,' the man replied in an expert's competent, sure-of-his-facts tone of voice. 'The light had been left switched on, and the wires had shorted, and started the fire. Once it had got going, of course, it didn't take long to spread.'

'I'll have it attended to. And in the meantime——' Earl thanked the man for his help.

'We'll finish up here, sir, and be on our way.' The fireman nodded in a friendly manner, saluted Roma, and took himself off, and she slid out of the Range Rover and ran to Earl's side, her face upraised, and her feelings mirrored in her eyes. It did not matter any longer that he saw how she felt, she did not care. All that mattered was that he was safe.

'Thank goodness you're all right,' she exclaimed joyfully. 'When you disappeared through that stable door, I thought . . , I was afraid. . . .'

His face was smeared with dark streaks of soot, his eyes were inflamed from the smoke, and a splinter of blackened wood, still emitting a thin stream of smoke, rested on the top of his hair. She raised her hand to brush it away.

'It's no thanks to you that any of this is safe!' He caught her hand in his own, reaching up to thrust her fingers away from his hair, and his grip was hard, and tight, closing round her hand with an angry force that made her gasp as much with the shock of his accusing words, as with his steely grip.

'Me? What have I got to do with the fire?' she cried, bewildered by his rebuff.

'Everything, if what the fireman said just now is true, and I've no reason to doubt it.' His voice vibrated with a savage anger that drained the blood from her face, leaving her eyes enormous in its whiteness. 'You knew the switch in the tack room was faulty,' he grated. 'Steve told you not to switch the light on when you went to fetch his jacket this morning.'

'I didn't switch it on. I could see well enough without it,' she cried defensively, but he brushed aside her protestations with an impatient wave of his hand, and went on harshly,

'You heard what the fireman said just now. The light was left on, and the switch shorted, and set the tack room on fire.'

'Someone else must have switched it on, after we left for the races,' she protested, her temper rising to match his own. Why should he blame her? There were other people besides herself around the stables, any one of them could have switched on the light, and forgotten about it.

'Why should they?' he enquired hardly. 'It was already full daylight when we left for Cheltenham. There would be no need for anyone to use the electric light after that. If this was your idea of revenge, because I told you to take Silver Cloud away from my stables, it hasn't succeeded,' he finished grimly.

'How could you suggest. . . .' Roma stared at him in stunned disbelief. How could he think, how could *anyone* think, she would do such a thing?

'I'll make you pay for every penny of the damage that's been done here today,' he thrust aside her angry denial. 'I'll make you pay,' he repeated, and his eyes glowed with the fury of the anger storm that rode him. 'If you can't find the money to pay for the damage, I'll take it out of the purchase price for the Lodge.'

'I haven't said I'll sell you the Lodge,' she began furiously.

'What choice will you have, now?' he asked her bitingly, and thrust her hands roughly away from him.

'Guv'nor, can you come and lend a hand, the bay's still playing up. . . .'

'Coming.' Earl turned and looked down on her as he swung away. His angry eyes seemed to pierce right through her, nailing her to the spot. Roma wanted to run after him, to make him listen to her, to make him believe her, but her feet refused to move. It was as if, she thought hopelessly, it was as if they knew it would be of no avail. She became conscious of cold, seeping through the soles of her shoes from the cobbles that still ran wet from the firemen's hoses, a black, sooty wet, that carried with it the acrid tang of destruction, and swirled pieces of charred wood and half burned paper into tiny dams in the gaps between the cobbles. A piece of paper touched the toe of her shoe, and she looked down at it with dull eyes. It still showed bright colour along its glossy edge, where the flames had not caught it. It was probably from the calendar that had adorned the tack room wall just above the light switch. The colour seemed to mock her, laughing at her desolation. She kicked the paper away, fretfully, and it swirled on in the tiny stream of water, dancing gaily towards the group of horses and men going out of the other end of the stable yard, just like the handful of straw had danced in between the hooves of the colts. She half expected the black kitten to appear, and chase after it.

'Satan?' She had forgotten about the kitten. Now she remembered, and felt sick. The last time she had seen the little animal, it had been curled up on Steve's jacket. She remembered lifting it up, and then putting it back down again on the chair cushion, a small, warm, sleepy bundle of black fur, that purred, and opened its mouth in a pink-tongued yawn, then settled down to sleep again on the tack room chair. And now the tack room was a disaster area, containing only the charred remains of its contents.

'Satan?' Her feet came to life, and sped her to the tack room door. Its blistered paintwork gaped wide, but the wood itself was curiously unscorched. Even as she ran through the opening, a detached part of her mind noticed that it was unscorched. A fireman straightened up from winding his hose, and looked at her curiously as she skidded to an abrupt halt inside.

'If you're looking for Mr Paget, miss,' he suggested, 'I saw him taking the horses out at the other end of the stable yard, not a few minutes since.'

'I don't want Earl.' She did, but not for any reason she could explain to the fireman. 'I'm looking for a cat. A young black cat.' She gulped to an unhappy halt.

'He'll be black and no mistake, if he's been among this lot,' the fireman surveyed his charred surroundings ruefully, and then he took a keener look at Roma's colourless face, and his voice changed. 'Your cat won't be in here, miss,' he assured her kindly. 'He'd take off for safer quarters the minute he smelled smoke.'

'He might have been trapped. . . .' She could not go on.

'There's no chance of that, miss. The door was hooked back when we got here, like it is now. One of the stable lads told me the door's always kept hooked back during the daytime.'

Which explained why the wood was only blistered, and not burned.

'I expect the fire bell frightened him away, and all the fuss and water,' the fireman suggested. 'Cats hate noise as much as they hate getting wet. He'll come back when everything's quietened down, you'll see,' he comforted. 'He'll come back when he gets hungry.'

'Yes. Yes, of course he will.' Roma was not sure whether she was agreeing with the fireman, or trying to convince herself. She could not visualise the stables without the black cat. She had got used to having it around, to including it in the fuss she made of Silver Cloud when she visited her horse each morning. The cat had become a kind of symbol to her. Black cats were supposed to be lucky, weren't they? After her visits became routine, it had got into the habit of stalking across the top of the stable door, surefooted as a tightrope walker, and jumping down into her arms, where it purred its content under her stroking fingers until something else took its attention, and it scampered off to play elsewhere. Cuddling it to her, she could almost make herself believe that everything would turn out well in the end, that the quarrels and mis-understandings between herself and Earl were only tem-porary, and they would, in time, sort themselves out. And now there was no time left. The grey filly would soon have to leave the stables, and its trainer. She would soon have to leave Burdon Court. And now there was no cat, either. No good luck symbol, to encourage her to persist in her rosy daydreams.

'Perhaps it's as well. I've got to face facts some time.' With bleak eyes she faced them. She still had to find a place for Silver Cloud. She still had to find a home for herself. And she could not possibly afford to keep the Lodge, now she had to pay for the fire damage to the stables. Her savings were already getting dangerously low.

'Why *should* I pay for the cost of the fire?' She jerked her thoughts to an indignant halt. 'It wasn't my fault that it happened.' She was as bad as Earl's staff, she told herself scornfully, accepting that she had to do this, or do that, just because Earl said so. It was high time somebody challenged his arrogant assumption that his word was everybody else's bond, she told herself determinedly. And it looked as if that somebody, her determination wavered slightly, it looked as if that somebody was going to be herself.

'I'm going to need a lucky charm when I tell Earl he's got to pay for the fire damage himself,' she told herself ruefully on her way to visit Silver Cloud the next morning. The trainer had not appeared at the dinner table the evening before, nor at breakfast, although she had not expected him to the early morning meal, he was usually up and out long before she came downstairs. When she got into the stable yard, he was not there, either, and neither was the black cat.

'Have you seen Satan anywhere?' she asked Steve. She would not ask him if he had seen Earl. . . .

'Not this morning, Miss Roma, but he'll be around somewhere, I expect. Whoa! Stand still, can't you?' Steve was busy, and not inclined to bother about black cats. 'The string's still jittery,' he frowned, 'what with young Jimmy, and that firecracker, and then the tack room fire straight afterwards, they haven't settled down yet.'

'You haven't got all the string out for exercise,' she noticed. 'Silver Cloud?' Her horse was missing from its usual place at the head of the string.

'Silver Cloud's leaving.' Bob, the stable lad, joined them, looking glum, and Roma swung round on him, her lips tightening ominously.

'Earl told you Cloud's leaving?' She stared at him incredulously, and her anger rose against the trainer. It was bad enough that Earl had told her to remove her horse from his stables. It was infamous that he should discuss their quarrel with a stable lad, an apprentice jockey.

'I'll never forgive him for that,' she told herself furiously. The details were probably common gossip among the stables by now. And herself probably a laughing stock. . . .

'The guv'nor didn't tell me, Miss Roma.' Bob looked at her in a puzzled manner. 'I could see it for myself,' he said in a concerned tone. 'Normally, Cloud licks out her manger and looks round for more, but this morning she's leaving. She hardly touched her first feed.'

'You mean . . .?' Roma stared at him, comprehension dawning upon her.

'Cloud's leaving her feed, miss. It's all the upset, I expect.'

'Have you checked . . .?' Steve began.

'I've checked all you told me to,' Bob assured him earnestly. 'I've looked the filly over for any signs of a pricked hoof or a rise in temperature, but there's nothing. Cloud seems to be in perfect condition so far as I can see, but she's still leaving,' he repeated worriedly.

'We won't take her out with the string today,' Steve decided. 'Give her gentle exercise by herself in the indoor ring, and then bring her back to the stables. Keep her rugged up, and I'll get the Guv'nor to have a look at her as soon as he's finished his stint in the office.'

That usually took about an hour of Earl's time after stables, Roma knew, so she felt safe from any confrontation with him for the moment. She ran a newly knowledgeable eye along the string of horses being prepared for exercise, and observed,

'The black colt's missing, too.'

'The black colt isn't leaving. He's left.' A grin split the apprentice jockey's young face.

'Left the stables?' Dismay swept over Roma, and she swallowed with a suddenly dry throat. 'Has Horace Blantyre taken his horse away?' If he had, it was her fault. She knew she had offended the black colt's owner, and this must be his answer, to remove it from Earl's stables. To spite her, through Earl. No wonder the trainer was angry!

'It wasn't Mr Blantyre who removed his horse, miss. It was t'other way round,' Bob began.

'Miss Roma doesn't want to hear stable gossip,' Steve said crushingly, but the apprentice jockey was obviously primed with his news, and could not resist a fresh audience.

'I don't see why not,' he stood his ground. 'Everyone else knows the Guv'nor's told Mr Blantyre to take the black away from Burdon Court.'

'*Earl* told Horace Blantyre to take his horse away?' That was the second time in a week he had done the same thing, Roma counted up. First her own horse, and now the black colt. If Earl goes on like this, she told herself critically, he'll soon have no more horses left to train.

'Yes, miss,' Bob answered her eagerly. 'It seems the Guv'nor took mortal offence at something the man said, and by all accounts he gave him a right dressing down, and told him to take the black away. He said he wouldn't train him no more,' he finished with ungrammatical relish.

'But what about Mick?' The jockey would miss out on the black's races, and the prize money they would bring him.

'Mick told me he wouldn't ride the black again for all the gold in the bank,' the boy replied with youthful candour. 'It seems he's as angry as the Guv'nor, and I can't say I blame him, I. . . .'

'You get on with your work,' Steve cut short his narration with an ominous scowl.

'Well, you did say yourself you wouldn't work with the black colt again, not after what Mr Blantyre said,' Bob answered defensively.

Roma felt as if her ears were deceiving her. Earl had tossed away a promising colt because its owner had insulted her. Mick had refused to ride it, and Steve to work with it, for the same reason. They had all three of them championed her at a loss to themselves. A small, warm glow started inside her as the knowledge penetrated.

'What I said, or what an owner said, makes no difference,' Steve rounded on the boy fiercely. 'Miss Roma isn't concerned with stable gossip. . . .'

'And I don't pay my staff to waste time repeating it!'

They all three jumped as Earl's voice came sharply from behind them.

'Go back to your work,' he ordered Bob abruptly.

'I've finished Silver Cloud, Guv'nor.'

'Then go and give Willy a hand with his grooming, he can't manage properly with a damaged wrist.' Earl sent the boy packing, and turned to Steve.

'Take the string to the gallops for a workout this morning,' he instructed the head lad. 'A bit of hard work will take their minds off fires and fireworks, and if they're tired they'll settle down more quickly.' He glanced along the string critically. 'Why isn't Cloud out?' He missed the grey for the first time.

'Bob's not satisfied with her condition,' Steve replied. 'He says she's leaving. As soon as I've finished with the bay, I'll check her over.'

'You carry on and take the string out, they're getting restless,' Earl decided. 'I'll check the grey.' He stood and watched the line of horses move off, then turned towards the stables.

'I'll come with you.' Roma stifled her qualms and fell into step beside him.

'There's no need.' His demeanour was the reverse of encouraging. He had championed her in public, but his attitude to her had not altered one whit in private, she thought, and the warm glow vanished, and left the familiar cold emptiness behind. He made no attempt to slacken his stride to allow her to keep up with him easily.

'There's every need. Cloud's my horse, and I want to know what's wrong with her.' She had to trot to keep up with him, which warmed her cheeks and her temper more with every step she took, but she was right at his heels when he opened the stable door. She slid in behind him, but in spite of her determination she had to nerve herself to look in Cloud's box when she got there. She did not know what to expect, and her stomach tightened with apprehension as she forced herself to look inside.

'She . . . looks just the same.' She let out her breath in a little puff of relief. And then some of the tension returned as she took a keener look at the filly. The grey was not the same. It was difficult to pinpoint what was wrong, but there was some indefinable difference in the animal. Roma knitted her brows as she studied it closely. The big grey head turned at her approach, and the filly blew gently through its nostrils as she stroked the silky nose. 'She seems to have . . . to have lost her sparkle.' It was the only way she could think of to describe it.

'I've checked everything I can think of, Guv'nor.' Bob's head appeared like a Chad above the dividing partition, from where Willy's tuneless whistle proclaimed that he was doing his best, despite his injured wrist, to carry out his task of grooming his mount.

'Tell me,' Earl spoke over his shoulder to the boy, while he talked gently to the grey, lifting up its hooves, examining each one in turn; going from point to point of the big body, his slender, sensitive fingers stroking, feeling, telling him what his eyes could not, while the apprentice jockey related what he knew, and what he thought. Earl listened to the stable lads, Roma noticed, weighing their opinion with his own, respecting the fact that each boy had sole care of a pair of horses, and would necessarily get to know the individual animals better than anyone else could hope to do.

'Hmmm. . . .' He stepped back at last, and Roma watched him with fearful eyes. What would his verdict be? Instinctively her hands went up to rub the horse's nose, seeking comfort for herself as much as seeking to impart it.

'Don't push,' she chided gently as the big animal nuzzled her arms, rocking her off balance. 'Cloud's looking for Satan,' she remarked wistfully over her shoulder to Bob, and lapsed into miserable silence, unhappy about the horse, worried about the cat, and wretched for herself.

' 'ere, Guv'nor, d'you reckon that's what's the matter with the grey?' In his excitement, Bob scrabbled higher up the dividing partition, hanging on by his elbows the better to put over his point. 'I never gave it a thought,' he chided himself, and clicked his tongue vexedly.

'What do you think is the matter? What is it, about the cat?' Earl questioned him, his glance suddenly keen.

'Well, Satan's gone missing since the fire,' the boy explained excitedly. 'It could be that the grey's pining.'

'It could very well be,' Earl agreed. 'So far as I can tell, there's nothing physically wrong with the filly, and if she *is* moping for the cat, the animal will have to be found and restored to her stable without delay, or the horse will begin to lose condition.'

'We can't let that happen, Guv'nor,' Bob protested vehemently, 'I'm riding Cloud in the Vintners' Stakes at the end of next week.' His face registered the potential disaster to his own career, as well as the grey's, if the horse lost condition, and consequently its chances of success in the all-important race.

'What can we do?' Roma fixed pleading eyes on Earl's face, mutely begging for his help, his reassurance. She got neither.

'There's only one thing *you* can do,' he told her bluntly. 'Go and search for the cat.'

'I'll go in one direction, if Bob will go in the other.' She poised, ready to fly off and search.

'Bob will remain in the stables, and get on with his work.' Unbelievably, Earl refused her. She stared at him, anger and consternation chasing one another across her mobile features.

'But. . . .'

'I've got other horses to look after besides yours,' he told her bluntly, 'and two stable lads temporarily disabled into the bargain.'

'It's not my fault they were injured,' she cried indignantly. Not even Earl could blame her for that.

'No matter whose fault it was, the results are the same. It means a heavier workload on the other stable lads, and I can't spare one to go on a wild goose chase after a stray cat.'

'You don't want the cat to be found.' Realisation washed over her in a sickening wave. 'You don't care if

Cloud loses condition.'

'You're talking nonsense. Hysterical nonsense.' He caught her roughly by the arm.

'It's far from nonsense, and I'm not hysterical,' she denied shrilly. She was. She felt hysteria rising in her like a water spout, protesting hysteria, that this thing could not be, that it must not be allowed to happen. Hopeless hysteria, that wanted to laugh out loud at the irony of it all, and weep even louder at the consequences. She grasped at anger to save her.

'You'll be glad if Cloud's out of condition for the Vintners' Stakes,' she stormed at him accusingly. 'You'll have the perfect excuse then, if she loses, and your own horse wins!'

'Stop it, Roma!' He gave her a shake that brought her spate of wild words to a gasping halt. She drew in a shuddering breath, but before she could speak again,

'You're talking nonsense, and you know it,' Earl grated harshly. 'Cloud's got the same chance in the race as Arabian Minty. Better, if anything, because her own lad will be riding her. Bob looks after her, Bob feeds her, and with Bob on her back she'll give of her best because she trusts him. That's why, with a young horse in its first season, I never put a strange jockey on its back if I can help it. It gives the animal confidence to be under someone it knows.'

'Cloud knows Mick.'

'Not so well as she knows Bob. He's looked after her since she first came to Burdon Court.'

He would not be looking after her for much longer. The reminder opened the floodgates of her bitterness once more.

'Then let him continue to look after her now,' she panted. 'Let him help me to find the cat.'

'It's your own fault the cat's missing.'

'My fault?' He still did not believe her. He still thought——

'You left the tack room light on.' His face, his voice, were hard, angry, and unforgiving, promising to exact the full penalty for what he believed to be her deliberate action. 'You knew the switch was faulty, and Steve told you it would short if you switched it on. You must have known what the consequences would be. Well, one of the consequences has rebounded on your own head,' he told her grimly. 'If the cat doesn't come back, and the filly continues to pine for it, she'll lose condition so fast she won't be fit to even be taken to the race, let alone to run in it. So find the cat if you can,' he thrust her away from him, as if even touching her was repugnant to him, 'find it if you can,' he repeated harshly, 'but look for it by yourself!'

'The fire in the tack room wasn't my fault,' Roma repudiated his blame with set lips and flashing eyes. 'If you don't believe me, I don't care.' She did, but she dared not let it show in front of Earl. Defiantly she raised her banner high and rushed into battle. 'I didn't leave the light switch on, and I won't be made to pay for the cost of a fire I didn't start. And as for the cat,' she rushed on heedlessly, before she could let herself think about how much she cared, 'I'll go and look for it by myself. You can keep your help, I don't want it. I'll find the cat, and bring it back, and . . . and. . . .'

Quite suddenly, the fire inside her went out, its bright, hot flame extinguished by the glacial anger in Earl's hard eyes. She turned blindly away from them and fled the stable, groping for the door before the sobs that racked her throat should burst from her trembling lips and shame her for ever in front of the trainer, and the two stable lads working in the next stall.

With feet that stumbled, and eyes that could not see for the scalding tears that flooded them, she ran, although in which direction she ran she could not tell, any more than she knew whether she ran to find the cat, or to get away from Earl.

CHAPTER TWELVE

THERE was not a nook or cranny that she had not searched. She even—she shuddered when she remembered the spiders—she even climbed the ladder from the feed room into the loft above it, and searched in the dim, cobwebby recesses of the roof beams, but her torch picked out no answering, luminous eyes, no frightened crouching bundle of fur, and in the end she returned to ground level, defeated.

'Have you found . . .?' Bob appeared in the feed room with a measuring bowl and a questioning look on his face.

'No, I thought Satan might have come back during the night,' Roma returned despondently. 'There's no sign of him.'

She had searched until dark, and then, when the strained evening meal had at last dragged to its close, she refused the coffee that Mrs Murray took as usual to the drawing room, and instead begged a glass of milk.

'I'll take it to bed with me, and have an early night.' She made her excuses and escaped thankfully from the room, but not to go to bed. 'I'd rather die with thirst than face Earl glowering at me from the other side of the fireplace.' She tried not to mourn her lost coffee, and fought down desolation because what might have been between herself and Earl was not—the sweet, warm oneness engendered by the firelight, and two people in harmony with one another. She dared not let herself think, 'in love.' The reality was so very different. She caught her breath on a sharp sigh at the difference, and made her way stealthily out of doors towards the stable yard. She reached it without being challenged, and bent to place the saucer on the cobbles outside Silver Cloud's box. 'This might tempt Satan back, if nothing else can,' she assured herself, and called softly, just in case, 'Puss! Puss! Puss!'

'You can't leave that there, it'll get broken.'

'Oh!' She straightened abruptly with a startled exclamation, and the glass of milk and the saucer dropped from her nerveless fingers and shattered on the cobbles at her feet. The milk felt cold as it splashed against her stockings. 'Now look what you've done!' She turned angrily on the tall dark shadow that spoke with Earl's crisp tones. 'Did you *have* to creep up behind me like a ghost?'

Her own face resembled one, its chalk white oval illumined only by two enormous, startled eyes. 'You've made me break Mrs Murray's glass and saucer!' she blazed at him, fright and nervous tension raising her voice high.

'Mrs Murray's kitchenware is of no consequence to me,' Earl snapped back, 'but the hooves of my thoroughbreds are. There's broken glass and crockery all over the stable yard!'

'Don't exaggerate.' She laughed his words to scorn. 'There's only a few small pieces. It was just a glass, and a saucer. . . .'

'Just one tiny piece is quite sufficient to prick a horse's hoof and cause it to go lame.' He swept aside her defence impatiently.

'If you're that worried, I'll pick up all the bits myself,' she began angrily.

'Leave them,' he bade her curtly, and caught her by the arm as she bent to search at her feet in the darkness. 'I'll alert the yard man to clear them first thing in the morning, before the string's brought out into the yard.' He steered her determinedly away from the stables, and in the direction of the house. 'It's nearly ten o'clock, and no time to be hunting for shards of crockery. It's a pointless exercise in the dark, in any case.'

'I wanted to leave a saucer of milk, in case Satan came back,' she defended her presence in the stable yard.

'Wherever the cat's got to, it's probably curled up asleep by now,' he cut her short. 'Which is where you led me to believe you were going, when you left the dining room. You said you were going upstairs to have an early night, and instead I find you creeping about in the dark in the stable yard.' He made it sound like a crime.

'It's not a crime,' she defended herself vigorously. 'But if you're so concerned about me trespassing in your precious stable yard, I'll leave you in sole possession. You're welcome to it,' she flung at him bitterly. 'You're welcome to all of it.' She meant it. She even meant the Lodge. She felt as if she did not want to see any of it, ever again. 'Good*night*!' she stormed at him, and swung her arm, trying to wrench herself free from his grip.

'Goodnight, Roma.' She was unsuccessful. She might as well have tried to break free from a handcuff as from Earl's steel grip. His fingers retained their effortless hold, and he swung her to face him, and bent his head above her own.

'Goodnight, Roma,' he repeated, and without warning his lips crushed down on hers with a swift, savage kiss that stifled her startled protest before it could be uttered. For a brief, agonising moment, that seemed to endure for an eternity of torment, his lips held her captive. A moment in which her heart beat with suffocating speed, racing with a wild longing that refused to be denied. If it went on for another minute—another second—she would be lost.

'I must be mad!' She started to struggle, as much against her own weakness as against Earl's iron hold. 'Let me go!' she panted, and thrust against him with balled fists. 'Let me. . . .'

Unexpectedly, he let her go. He released her suddenly, and she was caught unawares, and staggered backwards, off balance. Her fingers rose to cover her bruised and throbbing lips in an unconscious gesture of defence, as his voice mocked her through the darkness.

'Goodnight, Roma.'

'I hate you!' she choked. Hating him helped her to fight the weakness, and the threatened tears, and bolstered her courage to cry at him angrily, 'If you're thinking of guarding your stable yard against me, you needn't bother. I'm going.' She lashed out, trying to hurt him as he had inflicted hurt upon her. 'I'd rather stay in my own room for ever than suffer another minute of your company!' she shouted wildly, and without waiting for him to answer, she fled for the sanctuary of the house.

She ran through the hall, and gained the stairs; heard behind her Mrs Murray's mildly puzzled, 'Why, Miss Roma, I thought. . . .' But she did not wait to hear what Mrs Murray thought. She sped on across the landing, and burst into the blessed privacy of her own room, and slammed the door behind her, and leaned against it, her breast heaving, and her shaking limbs scarcely able to hold her upright. At last the trembling subsided, and she pushed herself wearily away from the door and dropped limply on to her bed, but not to sleep, and when eventually her sobs subsided in a restless doze, it was to feel again the torment of Earl's kiss. Daylight released her at last, and with a sense of relief she forced her mind on to the immediate necessity of finding the cat. She dressed quickly, and slipped outside before Earl could finish his breakfast.

'Perhaps Cloud will be so hungry that she'll eat anyway, this morning.' She followed Bob hopefully into the filly's box.

'No such luck, miss,' the lad dampened her hope. 'I thought I'd tempt her with a warm bran mash, but she doesn't want it.' The rich, warm, porridgy smell filled the stable, but the grey turned her head away from her manger, uninterested. An aura of dejection hung over the animal, and it responded half heartedly to Roma's approaches. 'Do you see what I mean, miss? She's leaving.' The boy looked as unhappy as the horse, and Roma's spirits dropped to match.

'I've looked everywhere for Satan. I've quartered the stables. . . .' She did not know where else to look, and she stared helplessly at Bob for inspiration.

'The Guv'nor'll be along soon, maybe he'll be able to think of something,' was all the lad could offer.

'I'll go and have another look, just in case.' Roma galvanised into action. To meet Earl now would be the last straw. The shards of glass and china were gone from the cobbles, she noticed, as she emerged from the stable, and cast a cautious look around the stable yard, wondering in which direction she should turn so that she might not bump into Earl. There was no sign of the trainer, but. . . .

' 'morning, Guv'nor.'

' 'morning, Steve.'

She was only just in time. Earl's voice came from the entrance to the yard nearest to the house. Roma hurried through the only exit left to her, on to the main drive. She hesitated when she reached it, then turned restlessly and walked in the direction away from the house. She did not want to go indoors again. She felt stifled, trapped, under Earl's roof.

'I'll go and see if my own roof's been repaired yet.' The idea appealed to her. At least it was something positive for her to do. Searching for the cat was an abortive occupation, she decided dejectedly, her spirits as grey as the early morning light. It was like searching for her own identity, an equally useless task. Since she met Earl, she seemed to have lost herself, revolving round the trainer like a satellite round the sun, and like a satellite, remaining always at a distance, unapproached, and unapproaching.

She reached the Lodge gate, and checked in surprise. In place of its sagging predecessor, a new gate swung smoothly on oiled hinges, part of a new post and rail fence that surrounded the garden which in turn looked—Roma eyed it with growing amazement—as if an army of workmen had been busy clearing the tangle, and reducing it to order. Fresh wallflowers edged newly planted borders, and young rose trees, their orange labels still attached and fluttering in the light breeze, promised summer glory to come.

'Earl hasn't wasted much time,' Roma muttered to herself bitterly. The trainer must be very sure of his ability to acquire the Lodge, whatever her own feelings in the matter, for him to have so much work done in the garden. It was not called for under the terms of the will, she remembered uneasily, under which only the structure of the Lodge itself had to be put in good working order. She raised her eyes to inspect the roof. That, too, was finished. Pale reed gleamed lightly, sheltering the windows and door with deep, perfectly shaped scallops, the work of a craftsman. New window frames bore fresh paint. One window had still to be glazed, she noticed. It gaped at her, sightlessly, and she regarded it with speculative eyes.

'I wonder if they've finished the inside of the cottage, as well?' If they had, it would be ready to move into, which would solve at least one of her problems. She tried to feel glad about it, but failed signally, and took refuge from her thoughts in practical action.

'If the door's locked, I might be able to get in through the window.' She tried the door. It was locked. A pointless exercise, she thought drily, since any intruder would have easy access through the window. A brand new shiny Yale lock gleamed at her from the freshly painted door, and the sight of it roused her to anger.

'No doubt Earl's got the only key in his possession. If it hadn't been for the window, I'd have been locked out of my own house!' The trainer would know that, doubtless rely on her going there, and finding herself locked out. Emphasising, without words, his mastery over herself and her possession. Her teeth clenched, so hard that they made her jaw ache. 'He shan't stop me from getting in,' she vowed. She judged the distance of the windowsill from the flagged path on which she stood. It was not all that high, and she was dressed in slacks. 'Here goes,' she muttered, and taking a firm grasp of the woodwork she swung herself up on to the windowstill and through into the room beyond.

'My goodness, what a mess!' The new paintwork was not as dry as it looked, and her hands, and the bottoms of her slacks' legs, were liberally daubed. 'Perhaps the painter will have some turpentine with him, he should be here to start work very soon.' She gave a grimace of distaste as she surveyed her sticky hands, then shrugged philosophically.

'I might as well have a look round before the workmen get here.' She toured the ground floor in growing wonder. In the living room the stone fireplace, a gem of its kind, had been cleaned and restored by hands that appreciated its beauty, as had the ceiling beams and floorboards, hewn from solid oak, and dark with years.

'They've even started on the stairs.' The workmen had done the first few steps, and started on the banisters, which were unique in that they descended in steps like the stairs themselves. 'They make lovely seats,' Roma decided, and perched herself upon the bottom one the better to look around her.

'It's small.' The cottage seemed minute after the spacious rooms at the Court. Claustrophobic, even. 'But it's plenty big enough for one. More than big enough,' she told herself firmly, and tried to ignore the bleak emptiness of it that seeped into her spirits, penetrating them like winter cold into old bones. She tried to visualise the cottage as it would be when it was furnished, and found she could not. There would be a fire in the stone fireplace, and herself sitting beside it. Alone. Her mind shied away from the thought.

'I should have waited until the workmen were here.' They would have brought with them the cheerful bustle of busy life, that would have scattered the shadows that seemed to lie about the deserted rooms, and, she suspected, lay as much in her own mind as in the empty house itself. It was not quite empty. A shadow darker than the rest crept slowly down the stepped banister rail above her, one silent step at a time. It reached the bottom one, and. . . .

'Satan! Heavens, you did give me a fright!'

Roma started violently and half rose to her feet, then sank back on to the banister again with a shaky laugh as the cat leapt from the rail on to her shoulder, and then, as it was accustomed to do from the top of the stable door, dropped into her arms, where it curled up and started to purr.

'I've been looking for you everywhere.' Everywhere but

in the Lodge, she realised ruefully. 'It was very inconsiderate of you to disappear like that,' she scolded gently.

'The same could be said about your own behaviour!'

Roma spun round as the front door of the Lodge was pushed open by an angry hand.

'If you must absent yourself at mealtimes, you might at least warn Mrs Murray first,' Earl criticised her hardly. 'She's wondering why you haven't been in for your breakfast this morning.'

Roma had forgotten all about breakfast. A glance at her watch confirmed that breakfast time was now long gone.

'I didn't think——' she began defensively.

'That's obvious,' Earl observed coldly. 'Any more than you thought before you broke into the Lodge through the window. From the look of your hands, and the legs of your slacks, most of the woodwork will have to be painted again. I'll take Satan from you, before the cat gets paint all over its fur.' He reached out and removed the animal from her arms. 'The paint probably contains lead, and if it marks the cat's coat and it tries to lick itself clean, it'll do the animal more harm than good.'

'I didn't break into the Lodge,' Roma denied spiritedly. 'You can't accuse anyone of breaking into their own home!'

'You could have asked me for the key, before you came along here.'

'I shouldn't have to ask for the key to my own house,' she flared resentfully. 'I should have been provided with a key of my own.' She would not admit that she had not known she intended to come and see the Lodge. That she had wandered in this direction on the spur of the moment, hardly knowing or caring where her restless feet should lead her, so long as they took her in any direction that led away from the Court, and Earl. 'Satan hasn't got any paint on his fur.' She hid her relief. She felt strangely bereft without the cat in her arms. The small, warm, purring body had been a comfort. Her lucky omen had been returned to her. And now—a stab of jealousy ran through her—the animal nestled just as contentedly in Earl's arms, purring as it had done in her own. Her eyes threw a challenge across at the trainer, in which antagonism and anger, and bitter resentment hardened their soft grey into blocks of ice.

'Eh, miss, but you've got yourself all daubed up, and no mistake!' Before Earl could answer, a cheerful voice turned them both to face a blue-overalled figure in the doorway, his denims liberally splattered with multi-coloured evidence of his trade, and a friendly grin on his face as he viewed Roma's plight. 'You'd best get busy with my bottle of thinners and a clean rag, and get that off.' He sorted around in his workbox and discovered a bottle of sharp-smelling spirit and a rag that might have once been clean, but to Roma looked in an even worse state than her hands.

'Yon cat's been hanging about here ever since yesterday,' the painter observed chattily. 'He looks too well fed to be a stray, though.'

'He belongs in the stables,' Roma answered him shortly. 'One of the horses is fretting because he's gone missing.'

'Best get him back there, then,' the workman suggested amiably. 'I was going along to the stables myself. I meant to bring a length of twine to work with me this morning, and forgot about it when I set out. It'll save me a journey back home if I can beg a length from your head lad, Mr Paget?' he threw an enquiring glance at Earl. 'I want it for. . . .' he launched into technicalities, and Roma ceased to listen, her attention absorbed in transferring the streaks of paint from her person on to the already many-coloured piece of rag. The last streak surrendered to her ministrations as Earl said,

'Steve can let you have as much twine as you need. I've got the Land Rover outside, I'll give you a lift, if you like.'

'Let me have your key, and I'll open the door for you,' Roma offered instantly. 'If you let go of Satan now, he might take off again, and I don't want another hunt to find him,' she suggested craftily, and knew with quick chagrin that her ploy had failed.

'You don't need a key to open the door from the inside.' The gleam in Earl's eyes told her he was well aware that she had made the offer, not for his benefit, but in order to obtain possession of his key, and mocked her because she had failed.

'You just turn the knob, like this, miss,' the workman gave her a demonstration she did not need, she thought sourly, but at least the man's presence in the Land Rover saved her from being alone with Earl on the journey back to the stables, and she flashed a triumphant look at the trainer as he was obliged to release the cat back into her possession to enable him to take the wheel. Roma slid out of the vehicle before he could retrieve her burden, and handed the little animal over to the delighted Bob herself.

'Thank goodness you've found him!' The apprentice jockey exclaimed his relief, and hurried with the cat into the grey's box. 'Where?' he threw the question over his shoulder.

'In the Lodge.' Roma followed him in through the door. 'He got in through an unglazed window.' And so did I, she reminded herself grimly, still smarting from her failure to obtain Earl's key.

'The grey's starting to eat already, miss. Look at her, now,' Bob crooned delightedly.

Roma looked, but her eyes did not see. Her mind saw only Earl, coming to lean over the door of the box, behind her. She knew that he was there. He did not speak, and she did not turn round; she did not need to, every nerve end of her throbbed with a raw awareness of his presence. His eyes felt as if they were boring a hole right through her back. In self-defence she used the only barb left in her quiver.

'I found the cat myself, I didn't need Earl's help,' she remarked deliberately, and flinched as she listened to her own words. She would always need Earl, and his help. There would never be a time when she could do without

it, or him, and in any case she had not found the cat, it
had found her, but she would die rather than admit it in
front of the trainer, she told herself fiercely. With an effort
she thrust aside her own need, and concentrated on that
of her horse. 'Perhaps Cloud will settle down in time for
the race,' she said hopefully.

'The filly hasn't been off her feed for long,' Bob comforted, 'and she's making up for lost time now,' he grinned
happily. 'She hasn't lost too much condition.'

She had more than regained any she had lost, by the
morning of the race. The horse looked the picture of
health, Roma thought proudly, and thrilled to the
charged atmosphere of the course as she waited beside
Earl in the owners' stand.

'The Vintners' Stakes is special.' Steve was a willing
informant, Roma discovered gratefully. 'There's always a
party afterwards, everyone connected with the race goes
along to help the winner to celebrate.' There was a party
atmosphere on the course already, a contagious aura of
festive high spirits that boosted her own to match.

'There's a big field,' Steve commented.

'Twenty.' She counted the runners on her race card.

'Traditionally there are twenty-one,' Earl commented
casually, 'but one horse has gone lame, and has had to be
scratched.'

'You haven't scratched Cloud from the race? Not
again?' How like Earl! she thought scathingly. How typical of him, to say nothing to her until they were actually
on the course, among the racing crowd, where he knew
that it would be impossible for her to make a public fuss.
A gust of anger rose like a storm in her, and she turned
on him, her eyes blazing. 'The horse was in perfect condition, and you said yourself the going on the course would
be good today. You said it would be ideal for her to run.'
She choked into angry silence.

'I haven't withdrawn Cloud.' Earl's glance was steely.
'This is the race I trained her specially for.'

'And of course, you wouldn't dream of scratching
Arabian Minty?' The last horse he would withdraw would

be his own, she thought bitterly, and her voice took on an edge that cut like an east wind blowing across the snow.

'Minty's sound enough,' Steve butted in. 'The horse that's been scratched is an outsider.'

The same could be said about herself. The fury died as suddenly as it had arisen, and she felt sick, and shaken, the artificial uplift infecting her from the excited crowd draining away, and leaving her feeling flat and lifeless. She was an outsider, and had no hope of ever being anything else so far as Earl was concerned. She could find another trainer for her horse, and remain among the racing world, but that was not what she wanted. It was Earl, and not Earl's world, her heart desired. Earl was the prize she coveted, and without him her horse, and the Lodge, and all that they stood for, held no worth for her. She turned stinging eyes on to the track, trying to pick out her own horse from among the line-up of runners. The grey's light colour made it easy.

'Cloud's quite close to the rail.'

'She's got a good position,' Steve assured her, 'she'll be running on the inside of the bends, and not too close to the rail so that she gets hemmed in.'

Earl's horse was in the centre of the line-up. It was difficult, Roma discovered, to identify the chestnut among the restless, jostling array of horses, many of similar colour, but at last she managed to pick out the black and orange of Mick's distinctive silks.

'They're off!'

The now familiar roar from the crowd. The familiar surge of excitement. The solid phalanx of racing animals that would soon thin out, leaving the serious contestants out in front, and the runners-up lagging behind. Bob held Cloud close to the rails.

'He's holding her back. . . .' Roma would never forgive the jockey, or Earl, if the grey was held back.

'The results of the Vintners' Stakes can make or break the start of Cloud's racing career.'

Vividly she recalled Earl's very words. Vividly it flashed across her mind like a bolt of fire, that Earl still had the power to destroy Cloud's future on the racecourse. Would he use that power, unscrupulously to break the horse—and herself? Had he instructed Bob to hold the grey back, to give his own horse a better chance of winning? To make sure she had no hope of winning the prize money, and therefore of being able to afford to keep the Lodge? She clung to the front of the stand with fingers that felt as if they must crack under the strain. The horses raced away from them round the first bend of the course. Earl raised his fieldglasses to his eyes, and she wished fervently that she had a pair herself. The racing field became an indistinct, anonymous blur, that rose to the first fence almost in unison. They landed, and a pattern began to emerge. One or two horses dropped behind as they raced on, the pace already beginning to tell after the first terrific spurt of speed, but still the grey clung close to the fence, running easily, neither falling behind, nor apparently gaining ground, so far as Roma could judge.

'Arabian Minty?' She screwed up her eyes, straining to pick out Mick's silks from the multi-coloured patches that were the jockeys.

'He's in the middle, towards the front.' Roma followed Steve's pointing finger, and managed to pick out the chestnut, still in the centre bunch of horses, and ahead of Cloud. The chestnut *would* be ahead of Cloud. Earl's horse *would* be the one in front. . . .

'He's instructed Bob to hold the grey back. I'm sure of it.' There was no doubt in her mind that the grey was not going full out, to the limit of its capacity. The pace was fast, but not nearly so fast as it had been at Auteuil, where the filly had exhibited a burst of speed when it raced clear of the loose horse that told Roma it had ample capacity in reserve now. She watched with angry eyes as the field approached the second fence. It was a water jump, wide as well as high, and it thinned out the field further still, so that by the time the third hurdle was surmounted the horses were well strung out, making it possible to identify each individual one without trouble.

'Cloud's still with them!'

'She's running well.'

But not well enough to get in front of Arabian Minty. Two horses from the original bunch that surrounded the gelding contested for the lead with Mick as they approached an open ditch. One of the rivals pecked on landing, and fell behind, but the other two ran on, with Cloud still hugging the rails a good length behind. One more fence, a short furlong of uphill incline, and they would be past the winning post.

'Cloud, come on!' Roma could not remain silent a moment longer. The shout of encouragement burst from her. She knew that it was useless, but she shouted just the same,

'Cloud, come on!'

The two leading horses rose to the last fence together. The grey was only half a length behind now, and gaining. She rose to the jump without effort, and landed true, but Arabian Minty's rival did not. Roma screwed up her eyes in an effort to see more clearly. The two leading horses were similar in colour, and too far away to see detail without fieldglasses, but the second horse seemed to jump awkwardly, crosswise across the hurdle, and when it landed it ran straight across the chestnut's path.

'Minty. . . .' Roma gave a gasp of horror. The two animals must surely crash. They could not miss. . . . With her sight sharpened by fear, she saw Mick crouch low in the saddle, kneeing his mount into a desperate leap sideways to get out of the way, but he had no chance. The other horse was too close, and they were both running at too great a speed. She saw the chestnut stagger.

'Mick . . . Minty . . . they'll go down!' She caught at Earl's arm. Without thinking, she clutched at him for support, or for reassurance, she did not know which and she did not care. 'They'll fall,' she whispered fearfully.

'No, Mick's managed to pull out of it.'

With a piece of brilliant riding, the little Irish jockey steadied his mount and ran clear, and spurted forward to try to make up for lost ground. In a daze, Roma heard Steve exclaim,

'Cloud's gaining!'

For a brief, paralysing moment, she had forgotten all about Cloud. Now, she stared. There was no need for her to shout, 'Come on!' The grey seemed to fly. The apprentice jockey on top of her simply sat still, and let his mount go. And how she went! Mick tried his best to catch up, but the action of the other horse had spoiled the chestnut's stride, and the short, uphill furlong left to the winning post was not long enough in which to recapture lost ground.

'Cloud's winning,' Roma gasped incredulously, and then, in a voice that cracked with excitement, 'Cloud's won!' The grey put all she had got into the short end sprint, and passed the winning post a full length ahead of her nearest rival. Arabian Minty. Earl's horse. . . .

Roma's face came alive with excitement, her eyes sparkled, and in an excess of jubilation she flung her arms round Steve, and hugged him.

'Cloud's won!' she exulted. She longed to shout it from the top of the stand, to shout it at Earl, but she did not quite dare. In spite of everything, her own horse had beaten his to the post, in a clear, decisive victory.

'Cloud's won!' She expended her delight upon the head lad, instead.

'I dunno, miss. . . .' Steve's face expressed doubt, and she stared at him in disbelief. 'There could be a stewards' enquiry,' he said doubtfully.

'A stewards' . . . what?' The light went out of Roma's face, and her arms fell to her sides.

'The Guv'nor ought to make a complaint to the stewards over Minty getting bumped like that. Minty was all set to win.'

'Complaint? Stewards' enquiry? What on earth are you talking about?' Roma spun to face Earl. 'There's nothing to enquire about,' she denied hotly. 'Cloud won. She passed the post a full length ahead of Minty. You saw her yourself.'

'Just the same. . . .' The head lad still looked doubtful.

'Will you lodge an objection to the result, Guv'nor?' he asked.

How could the head lad even *ask* such a question? Roma wondered indignantly.

'No.'

'But. . . .' Steve began to protest.

'It was an accident.' Earl's tone was clipped, decisive, and brooked no argument. 'I saw it quite clearly through my field glasses. The other horse slipped as it took off, and turned sideways across the jump into Minty's path. It couldn't be avoided. That's the luck of racing.' He looked down at Roma as he said it, and there was the same enigmatic quality in his stare that made her suddenly unable to meet it. Uneasily she lowered her eyes, dropping her lashes across them as a barrier between herself and the thing she could not understand in his.

'It's time to go.' Earl took Roma's arm with a firm grip, and she went with him in a daze. His unexpected refusal to lodge an objection took the fire from her anger, and left her feeling confused, and uncertain, and curiously deflated. Silver Cloud had passed the winning post first. But had she won? The question rose to plague her. If it had not been for the incident at the last jump, would not Earl's horse have won instead? Half formed doubts and unanswered questions raced round and round in her mind, and Earl had to put her hand to the grey's leathers when they got to the winners' enclosure.

'It's your turn to lead in this time.' He brought her back to earth, watching her with a face that was expressionless, but with eyes that were not. She looked away, fiddling with the rein so as to avoid his stare, because of what use were expressions when you could not read them? As if in a dream she heard herself congratulate Bob on his success. The thought crossed her mind that it was the apprentice jockey's success, and not her own.

'He ran a good race.' Mick joined them, magnanimous in defeat.

'He ran a *great* race.' Unexpectedly, so was Earl. Roma raised startled eyes to his face, not expecting such a re-

sponse from the trainer. A detached part of her consciousness noticed that the scratch that marred his cheek
at the previous race had disappeared, the clean, healthy
tan on his skin showing no sign of its encounter with
the bramble patch.

'Lead Bob in,' he reminded her of her duty, 'he's waiting.'

This was to have been her moment of triumph, the
moment she had lived for all these weeks, and now it had
come she felt curiously flat, and desperately alone. She
did not pause to consider. She reached out her hand and
grasped Earl's sleeve, and her eyes on his were wide with
mute appeal.

'Come with me?' she begged.

He came, but he deliberately walked a little to one
side, leaving her to face the battery of cameras alone.

'Keep it up, Miss Roma, you're doing fine,' Bob encouraged her from the saddle as she flinched away from
one particularly persistent newsman and his flashing
camera.

She could not keep up the pretence for much longer.
Congratulations showered upon her from all sides. Her
hand was shaken by people whose faces her misty eyes
could scarcely see, and she afterwards could not remember. Through a haze she heard herself reply to the
congratulations, and somehow she kept the strained smile
fixed to her lips as she held out her hands for the trophy.

It was a cup. Large, ornate, and silver. And it felt icy
cold in her fingers. As cold as the thought that numbed
her mind, and nearly stopped for ever the painful throbbing of her heart.

'I've won the race. And lost the prize.' The only prize
she wanted. The only prize she would ever want. Earl. A
sideboard full of silver cups could not make up for the
bleak and inescapable fact that she had lost Earl.

CHAPTER THIRTEEN

EARL took the silver cup from her hand when they reached the room where the celebration party was being held, and placed it carefully on a centre stand reserved for it in the middle of a laden buffet table.

'Now to fill it.'

He bent down and picked up a bottle of wine from a crate which stood, surprisingly, right in front of the buffet table, instead of behind it, in full view of the room. The cork popped with the unmistakable sound of a champagne bottle, and to the accompaniment of a cheer from the guests, a stream of sparkling wine flowed into the waiting trophy.

'The crate of champagne is part of the prize to the winner of the Vintners' Stakes,' Steve took pity on Roma's look of surprise.

'You mean that crate of champagne belongs to me?'

'All of it,' the head lad grinned.

And Earl was calmly appropriating the entire crateful, as if it belonged to him. Roma's cheeks flamed.

'It's usual to ask, before you make free with other people's property,' she flared angrily.

'It's traditional for the champagne to be handed round at the party after the Vintners' Stakes,' he retorted with a straight look, and continued to deliberately open another bottle. 'You have the privilege of the first taste.' A privilege, to taste her own champagne? Roma choked on the first sharp sip, but before she could give voice to the angry retort that trembled on the tip of her tongue, Earl added, 'Afterwards, the other owners and trainers and the jockeys have a glass each. They shared in the race, and traditionally they share in this part of the prize.' Imperturbably he signalled to the hovering waiters to begin charging their trays of glasses from the now brimming trophy.

'It was a good win.' A tall, rangy man raised his glass in Roma's direction. 'Here's to the grey filly's future—and your own,' he toasted, and his eyes twinkled in a friendly fashion.

'Meet Liam Massey.' Earl called across a casual introduction. 'He's got a training establishment in Cumberland.' He broke off as a waiter approached to speak to him, and Roma frowned. Was there any significance in Earl making the introduction? she wondered suspiciously. Was he, without words, underlining his order for her to remove Silver Cloud from his stables?

'Well, that's fine by me,' she told herself hotly. She was looking for another trainer for the grey, and the celebration get-together provided just the opportunity she needed to meet up with one. No trainer should be averse to taking on a two-year-old that had just won the Vintners' Stakes.

By a fluke? The question rose again, uneasily, in her mind. Unanswerable. She took a deep breath, and turned to the rangy Irishman with a smile.

'I was looking for. . . .' she began.

'Earl? He was dishing out the champagne a second ago, but where he's disappeared to now, I can't . . . ah, here he is, coming round the table behind you.' The newcomer misunderstood her, and immediately made it impossible for her to finish her request by adding, 'You've got the finest trainer in the business for your grey, Miss Forrester. In Earl's hands, your horse can't lose.'

'I'll have to find someone else to take Cloud,' she realised with a sinking heart, and scanned the sea of faces with anxious eyes. Any one of the crowd might be the trainer who would take the grey, but which one? She had no means of knowing who were the trainers and who were the owners. The jockeys, at least, she could tell by their size. The noise and heat seemed to press down on her, clouding her ability to think clearly. With a desperate effort she tried to shake her thoughts into some kind of order. She must keep a clear head to think, to make plans. A small orchestra in a corner of the room competed with the noise made by the chattering guests, and she put her

fingers to temples that suddenly began to throb. 'It's so
hot in here,' she murmured, conscious that her companions were looking at her with evidence of concern.

'Come with me on to the balcony. We can get a breath
of fresh air there.'

Masterfully Earl took her by the elbow and steered her
through the crowd.

'I can't, I must stay here. I don't want. . . .' Roma
tried to protest, but the words trailed away unheard amid
the cheerful noise around them, and in spite of herself she
found her feet taking her along with Earl, away from the
room, and the crowd, and the noise. She *did* want, her
heart protested vehemently. She wanted Earl. She wanted
every single precious second with him until. . . . She tried
to close her mind to what must come after. Numbly she
allowed him to guide her through the double glass doors
at the end of the room that led on to a narrow balcony,
fringed with shrubs, and offering the merciful benediction
of silence, and cool air. Roma took a deep, steadying
breath. Tiny pinpricks of light already gleamed through
the early dusk, and behind them, following them through
the balcony doors, the sound of a flute rose, piercingly
sweet.

'Love me. Love me for ever. . . .'

She caught her breath on a sharp note of pain. The
music was speaking for her, pleading for her, but Earl
was deaf to its entreaty. Deaf to her own fierce longing.
He turned and closed the doors behind them, shutting
out the sound, and there was only the occasional faint
hum of a car engine coming from the town, muted by
distance and the hovering night, and her own quick,
panting breath that fluttered in and out through her
parted lips like a frightened bird.

She felt herself begin to tremble, and she stepped swiftly
to the corner of the balcony and leaned against the hard
stone of the balustrade for support, gripping its cold
roughness with desperate hands. Earl followed her. She
heard his footsteps approach from behind her, firm and
deliberate on the marbled floor. In another second he

would be beside her. She spun round to face him, her hands reaching out defensively as if to prevent him from coming any nearer, and words burst from her lips, the first words that came into her head, to use as a barrier between them.

'You used all the champagne. All of my prize.' She did not care about the prize. She felt as if she hated champagne.

'All except the one bottle,' he agreed gravely, and deliberately put his hands on the coping behind her, one on either side of her, hemming her in. She turned frantically to escape him, but his arms were steel bars, imprisoning her. Closing round her. She gave a gasp. His hands left the cold stone and grasped her, drawing her inexorably towards him. 'I've been so busy giving away your champagne, I haven't had time to congratulate you properly on your win,' he murmured.

'Don't mock,' her wide, frightened eyes entreated him. 'Don't mock.' The torment was too great to bear. Her courage failed, and she quivered under his touch, trembling uncontrollably. For a long moment he stared down at her, until it seemed as if she must drown in the deep, peat pool of his eyes, and then he bent his head. She tried in vain to wrench herself away, but with one arm he held her still, and with his other hand he cupped her chin in his fingers and turned her face up to meet his. She closed her eyes and swayed, half fainting, her body pliant in his arms.

'Congratulations on your win,' he murmured, and touched her lips lightly with his own.

'Don't! I can't bear it,' she cried brokenly. 'If you don't love me, for pity's sake don't kiss me!' The words were wrung from her, anguished, pleading, wild with pain. A sob broke from her trembling lips, and she felt him go suddenly still. It was like the stillness before a mighty storm—brooding, electric, and charged with tension. For a long, endless moment he remained still, and then he moved, and the storm broke over them.

Like a mighty whirlwind it engulfed them both, blowing away the pride, and the anger, the resentment and the fear, and burning it in an overpowering, lightning flash of passion that fused their lips as one. Roma clung to him, shaken and breathless, but exulting in the storm, laughing in the face of the tempest from the secure, warm shelter of his arms, His lips travelled on, demanding, receiving; seeking, finding; mutely questioning, and silently receiving her answer in a language more eloquent than words, blazing a trail of rapture that was no longer dangerous, because it was a trail they walked together, and would follow together for the rest of their days.

Earl's lips wandered, slowly, savouring the moments. They touched her dark fringed lids, and opened her eyes to the rapture. They found the tip of her ear where it showed below the curly cap of her hair, and bade it listen always to the piercing sweet message of the flute,

'Love me. Love me for ever. . . .'

And then they rested at last in the soft, throbbing hollow of her throat, sweetly perfumed with the essence of flowers, his own gift of fragrance from Paris.

'I love you, my darling. I love you.' His voice broke, and his eyes, the deep brown peat pools of his eyes, pleaded for him, their message clear at last. 'Marry me, Roma,' he begged her hoarsely.

Someone opened the balcony door, and the notes of the flute returned to haunt them.

'Love me. Love me for ever. . . .'

Roma did not see who it was who came. Perhaps it was the rangy Irishman with the twinkling eyes, who had toasted, 'The filly's future—and your own.' Whoever it was paused for a moment, and then turned silently away, pulling the door to behind him. It did not quite close, and the notes of the flute stayed with them, and Roma lifted her lips to Earl's, letting the music answer for her, letting him read in her shining eyes the message that made her low-voiced murmur sweetly unnecessary.

'I love you. I'll always love you.'

'I've known no peace since we first met,' he confessed, when the storm passed at last, and she lay back against him, her head on his shoulder, quietly, like a bird come to rest. 'The first time I saw you, in the Lodge garden, I loved you. . . .'

The Lodge garden. It seemed like a lifetime ago. 'You didn't want me to live in the Lodge.'

'I wanted you to live in the Court, as my wife.'

'You can have the Lodge for one of your staff.'

'I don't want it. I had it restored to please you.'

'The men have nearly finished their work. It'll be ready for occupation soon.'

'Rent it out. It'll give you some pin money. Maybe Steve will have it, I know he's courting.' Earl's voice said he did not care either way. 'As soon as the men have finished on the Lodge, they'll start to repair the fire damage to the stable block.'

'I didn't set your stables on fire.' She turned wide grey eyes up to his, candid eyes, that said he must believe her.

'I know,' he confessed. 'Sean and Willy were working with Bob in the loose box next to Cloud's, and they heard me shout at you. They owned up. I'd have told you earlier, but we haven't been alone for more than a few minutes since then.'

'Surely Sean and Willy didn't . . .?'

'Not deliberately,' he calmed her anxious look. 'They tried to do me a good turn and mend the tack room switch themselves. I'd excused them stable duties because they'd been hurt, and I suppose they found time hanging heavy, but unfortunately they're no electricians,' he said with a rueful smile. 'They joined the wrong wires together. Mercifully they came to no harm themselves,' he put first things first, 'and the stables can be repaired.'

'Fog, and fire, and bolting horses,' Roma murmured wickedly. 'Life at the stables isn't exactly a peaceful affair.'

'But you'll share it with me? Promise you'll share it with me?' he begged her urgently, still unsure.

'I'll share it with you.' She wanted no other. She silenced his doubts with soft lips, and when at last, a long time later, she managed to set his fears at rest, he admitted,

'I was so afraid, the day the bay colt bolted. You stood right in its path.'

She had been wrong to assume that nothing could make Earl afraid. He had been frightened then, but for her, not for himself.

'Jimmy didn't mean any harm.' A faint pucker creased her forehead, remembering the young apple scrumper. Earl had been hard with the boy in the Lodge garden. He had threatened to punish him, justifiably, for throwing the firework. But . . . did he, perhaps, not like children? A shadow settled on her face at the possibility that he might not like children. 'Don't be too hard on him,' she begged. Suddenly it mattered how hard with the boy Earl intended to be. 'It was only mischief. He didn't think.'

'Jimmy will learn to think, now.' Incredibly Earl grinned. 'His father's bringing him to the stables to do a stint of work each Saturday morning. The lad's apparently been begging for the chance to come, for some time, and his father refused him because he thought he was too young. Now it'll keep him occupied, and earn him some pocket money, and when he learns more about the horses it'll give him a sense of responsibility towards them. I've tipped Steve off to let him know, casually, of course,' Earl's grin widened, 'that if he behaves himself, he can learn to ride. We've got a couple of mares too old for stud purposes, but I'm loath to get rid of them, I've had them since I started the stables, and a bit of gentle exercise in their retirement won't do them any harm.'

'Jimmy won't mind his punishment,' Roma laughed, a merry sound that held relief as well as happiness.

'All boys get into mischief,' Earl said seriously. 'At least, if they've got any spirit, they do. Our sons will get into mischief one day.' The glow in his eyes brought the soft, shy rose colour flooding to her cheeks, but she met his smile bravely, confident in their shared happiness.

'Perhaps they'll learn to ride Cloud, when she's too old for racing.'

'Cloud brought us together,' he remembered softly, 'we'll never let her go.' He settled the grey's future to both their satisfaction. 'Which reminds me,' he turned towards the door, his arm close about her, 'we mustn't forget to collect that bottle of champagne I saved from your prize.'

'We needn't bother. Let the guests have it.' She did not need champagne. The effervescent happiness that flowed through her veins was more potent than any wine.

'I saved it to toast our engagement.' Earl made it suddenly necessary to rescue the bottle of champagne.

'I kept it back for you, sir, like you said.' The head waiter handed it to Earl, ready wrapped in tissue paper. 'And I've dried out your silver cup, Miss Forrester, it's ready for you to take home.' He broke off, and raised his voice, thinking she had not heard him. 'Miss Forrester, don't forget to take the silver cup with you. Don't forget your prize.'

'I won't,' Roma promised happily. But her eyes were not looking at the silver cup. They were looking at Earl.

ROMANCE

Variety is the spice of romance

Each month, Mills & Boon publish new romances. New stories about people falling in love. A world of variety in romance—from the best writers in the romantic world. Choose from these titles in November.

WEDDING IN THE FAMILY Susan Alexander
BLUE DAYS AT SEA Anne Weale
HEARTBREAKER Charlotte Lamb
FIRST LOVE, LAST LOVE Carole Mortimer
TIGER MAN Penny Jordan
DREAM HOUSE Victoria Gordon
THE SPOTTED PLUME Yvonne Whittal
MY DEAR INNOCENT Lindsay Armstrong
THE JUDAS KISS Sally Wentworth
BITTER HOMECOMING Jan MacLean

On sale where you buy paperbacks. If you require further information or have any difficulty obtaining them, write to: Mills & Boon Reader Service, PO Box 236, Thornton Road, Croydon, Surrey CR9 3RU, England.

Mills & Boon the rose of romance

'Everyone loves romance at Christmas'

The Mills & Boon Christmas Gift Pack is available from October 9th in the U.K. It contains four new paperback Romances from four favourite authors, in an attractive presentation case:

The Silken Cage	– Rebecca Stratton
Egyptian Honeymoon	– Elizabeth Ashton
Dangerous	– Charlotte Lamb
Freedom to Love	– Carole Mortimer

You do not pay any extra for the pack – so put it on your Christmas shopping list now.
On sale where you buy paperbacks, £3.00 (U.K. net).